RP And Persephone's Pup:
The Glyphs Emerge

RP went to hell. Winter came and went, spring popped through the ice and damn near swamped the ship he'd parked too close to the glacier above, well Glacier. He'd gotten himself stuck between realities and couldn't decide if he liked this dimension or if it were hell, really.

And there she was, seventeen travel trunks crammed with everything she'd need for the winter season. Doggie treats from Dee O Gee spilled out of a carry-on with thirty cases of sparking water crushing the edge of the canal. Was that a canal? Some weird dude dressed like a Halloween death eater sat stoically in a shift. His gnarled hand lightly grasping

the silver boat catch, no wind, no nothing actually.

"Damn she's a looker," RP said under his breath.

"And who might you be?" The goddess in white broke silence like a warm wind grazing the cheek.

"Who, me?" Attempting to straighten his off-world garment, he checked for stains and chunks of Keetisd Pie that might have missed his mouth.

"Oh, well, I'm RP." He stuck out his hand only because it seemed the correct thing to do.

The goddess rolled her eyes and looked behind her for something.

A REALITY PIRATE ADVENTURE

"Have you seen a three-headed puppy? I told him I'd bring down some jerky and toys. I know he's here, he's always at the dock waiting for me." She turned all the way around and peered into the black abyss over the river.

"What is a dog doing here anyway?" tried RP, inching closer to the Jasmine scent wafting off her long dress.

"This place super sux. What's a goddess like YOU doing here?"

RP shapeshifted into one of his best superhero forms to impress.

"Forgot your foot." she giggled.

RP looked down at his left foot, horrified to see it still sporting his Pleiadian green tennies and orange sock begging a fresh wash.

"Damnit!" he focused harder, managing to morph it into the slick black loafer of 1970s fashion.

"Well, that's certainly more attractive." She adjusted her gown, offering a heady second wave of Jasmine.

"I come here half of the year because I'm supposed to. Winter and all, you know. It's not so bad once you adjust to the

Look for our illustrated book collaboration coming soon!

fell in is the River Styx. Charon will introduce himself perhaps. I'm Persephone. Welcome to Hell."

RP almost threw up on her feet. He'd not managed to navigate this poorly in years. Well, if you discount the swallowing of the dragon egg and all that dimensional shit. No, this was bad. Terrible in fact.

A concordance of thumping rang through the chamber, sounding like mittens loaded with rocks. Persephone squealed

awfulness and the heat. I bring D3 capsules too…"

"All right, enough of this." RP backed up and almost fell into the river, returned now to the RP we all know and love.

"I think I'm in the wrong dimension or whatever. To hell with this."

"You're correct there, little man." She smiled and spread her arms wide.

"Welcome to Hell, THE hell of all times and places! That murky water you almost

with delight, throwing herself wholeheartedly into the carpet of flying fur with three heads. The slobber flung onto RP's coat and freshened the ground with puddles of delight.

"Cerberus! Oh Bee Bee! I missed you so much!" she sang into the cacophony of gurgles and grins. If one four-hundred-pound Mastiff could show love, three poured into one body exceeded all expectation.

RP froze. He feared he'd wet himself but thank whomever he was merely slobber-soaked through and through.

"Oh my GOD!" he yelled, trying to scrape slime off of his fav pants. But he stopped short realizing all eyes, all eight eyes, were on him.

Persephone's face paled. Cerberus stood ready to attack.

"You can't say that, that WORD, that name, down here!"

Cerberus lifted his huge leg and perfumed the river. RP stood like a good boy, praying to the unnamed deity that he wasn't lunch. Something resembling a smile appeared on Charon's face. Cerberus farted, increasing the sulphuric perfume of the place exponentially.

"Look," acceded Persephone. "I don't know why you're here but I'll tell you this...Hell is nothing to pussyfoot around. Thoughts become things, real things, as soon as you add emotions."

"So, this is the Astral realm?" RP calmed and took a greatly needed deep breath. " I

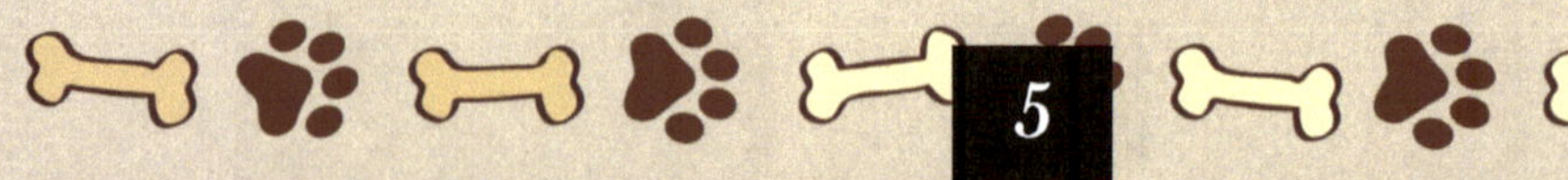

mean, the only place that happens is in the Astral."

Cerberus yawned and stretched out a humongous paw to get Persephone's attention. The water buffalo jerky she brought was his favorite "Up There" delight. She started bringing it down two thousand years ago. He thought it used to taste better but humans had mucked up the genetics and...

"Cut it out, Bee Bee!" Persephone peeled the hefty paw off her leg and gave him the look. He sat down obediently, loosening a gallon of drool from three mouths.

"All right, you've been such a good boy waiting for me to come back." She patted the head closest to her while opening the jerky bucket with the other hand.

RP watched with caution, trying to put everything here in some sort of historical perspective. He recalled Earth's ancient myth about Hades falling in love with Persephone while she clearly had no attraction to that type. Is truth stranger than fiction? I mean, there she is.

A putrid breeze wafted up from the river which, by the way, appeared slimier and more pungent than when RP had arrived. He turned towards the skiff but the Boatman was nowhere to be found. The iron dock was empty save for a few leg chains and flask of some awful liquid crawling with wormy things.

"Looking for me?" the voice surrounded RP like a wet black sheet coiling around his body. He attempted a step back but was met with a snarling middle head smelling like a cow hoof chew stick.

"Oh nope, not me, nothing like that." R P managed a slight step to the left. "I was just kinda, you know, wondering where…"

"We don't like the undead down here," snarled the Boatman. "You don't follow the rules and don't appreciate the vast expanse of the Hell venues."

The Boatman appeared to grow in height, his yellow eyes piercing what was left of RP's courage. "You care to take a little ride down the Styx? She can be awfully nice this time of year." He said, attempting something mirroring a smile.

RP cleared his throat and his head. A boat ride in Hell? Cement boots and no cell phone? No thank you, but he couldn't say that to Charon. I mean, the dude is a million years old. Can he even drive?

"I can hear you thinking. Is my offer not up to your standards, wherever it is you are from?"

"Fine, okay, whatever." RP adjusted his clothes and followed Charon to the water's edge and into the waiting skiff. Persephone sat on her trunk, hands languidly caressing six ears as equally as she could. Her smile resembled the Mona Lisa, sweet and undefined.

The murky water appeared anything but liquid. Was that oil? Was that even real? He sat on the tiny bench and dared a glance back at the boatman. Was he humming? Maybe the dead do sing.

The Boatman slipped silently into the main channel, if that's what it was. Nothing made sense down here and he regretted falling asleep and forgetting to set the Returnometer before his nap. So here he was, in Hell.

The river rose and fell like it was breathing. He couldn't see any shoreline or structures. Surely nothing living could

survive in this muck. Oh wait, he was the only living thing down here.

How much time had passed and where the hell were they? Surely, he could say hell in Hell. RP felt weird. He was hangry, wet, and hot. His feet hurt and his eyes stung from the sulphur perfumed air.

"Here we are," announced Charon.

The skiff magically appeared to float in the air above a vast endless desert of blackened bombed out buildings and burning skeletal cars. Fiery craters and literati looking trees hung silently in view. But where were the souls? You know, the evil ones sent here?

Looks like Beirut back in… but RP's reverie was halted when the skiff landed on a dock made of lead.

"Where are the people, I mean the souls?" RP addressed the Boatman.

"Are you surprised, alive man? No one's here except in their own mind. Their Astral body retains the seed atom and holds them to their own beliefs, no matter what they are." Charon knelt down and appeared to take a rest. Why would he need to do that, wondered RP?

"Just to see what you'd say." replied Charon.

Great, mused RP, another mind reader. But words seemed to calm him so he said, "If people send themselves here, why can't I see them? Where are all the people souls?"

"You still don't get it, do you?" Charon stood up. "They're here in their own minds, generating their own hell experiences. We provide the landscape, that's it."

"And where's Satan?" RP just knew he had him on that. After all, Hell was Satan's place. Hadn't Hades brought Persephone down here? RP was confused.

A REALITY PIRATE ADVENTURE

"After the Earth world wars, remember one and two were really just one war hiding between each other, Satan was sent back to Saturn on October 17, 1949. He's not even around any more, but the seven deadly sins are still an available download. He's not even on Earth any longer, used up all his karma cards. Hades, Satan, Pluto, whatever. Not here. But don't spread that around, it's bad for business."

"So, why'd you bring me here?" RP was more tired, more hangry than before. "What's the point?"

Charon stared at him for a moment before saying, "The correct question is why did YOU bring yourself down here?"

The question hung in the air like a Damoclean sword. RP shifted his feet, trying to appear in control. Charon stared at him and began again.

"What do you imagine Hell is, little guy? Could there be arcane parts of your being you could excavate to uncover the real RP?"

"You mean stuff like why I'm always hungry? I have no idea why, but I am." He shifted uncomfortably.

Charon gave him the side eye before continuing.

"Yes indeed, little guy. Imprints like that."

"I'm not little and I'm not a guy!" RP quit fidgeting and pulled himself up to his full 5'2", alarmed at the growing figure next to

him. Charon was growing. RP stepped back and almost fell into the black river.

"It's been 3,000 years since I could do that," said the 50' figure.

"Feels rather wonderful." If Charon could smile, the face now speaking 50' above RP was certainly attempting to display a satisfaction of sorts.

"Well, that's just rude!" yelled RP as he grasped the slimy skiff bow. Black ooze squished through his fingers, keeping him from regaining his balance or releasing his grip. RP plopped down on the dock, watching the huge figure shrinking back into its former 6' self. The boatman set down his pole and moved to the other side of the skiff, eying RP with a modicum of kindness.

"I'm not the monster you people think I am." He began.

"And I'm not a people!" RP was still yelling, he realized. But he was scared. The peculiar atmosphere of Hell was getting to him more than he wanted to admit. The signature of uncertainty weighed on his fear.

"Nothing like home." he mused, trying to think happy thoughts.

"What was that?" Charon interrupted his reverie. "Where is home?"

"Nowhere near here, that's for sure." RP said to no one in particular. His growling stomach and irascible mood did nothing to alleviate the hopelessness he now felt.

"Ow!" he yelled, grabbing his left hand from the slobbery cold mouth of the middle canine head. "Let go, beast! I thought you stayed back there with her." RP glared at Cerberus' one head calmly chewing on something resembling a lizard, the other two heads licking their lips with enough slobber to drown an army.

The Boatman began speaking, his voice taking on the amber calm of a wizened being sure of his place in the scheme of things.

"Let me tell you some things about this frequency and why Pluto really grabbed Proserpina from her mother's control. The myths claim Persephone, as you call her, was abducted and victimized by Pluto, damning her to living half of the years in Hades. But no one mentions the fact of her being 26 years old, during her first Saturn Return when the theme of that time is always a scheduled crisis of change and coming of age. Persephone just had to grow up. She'd been coddled and cuddled by her over protective Mother, Ceres, for the allotted time. They never really got along anyway. Remember, Saturn rules time. She was given a truly Plutonic experience when the underworld grabbed her, forcing the

unexpected discomfort of change that awakened Proserpina to her true purpose."

"And exactly what was THAT?" interrupted a perturbed RP.

"I'm getting there." Charon picked up his staff seemingly to add import to his words.

"Proserpina's true purpose was and is to show what the immature, personality of the feminine must undergo to become the Divine Feminine. She married Pluto, see? She literally joined equally with the underworld, unseen, subconscious aspect of Divine Femininity. If she'd not done that the 2,500-year cycle of the Divine Feminine would not be offered to both masculine and feminine during these particular years. All cycles and returns to itself."

The giant three headed pup was snoring loudly from a ways down the dock. Giant drool slobbers blew frothy bubbles with each exhale, predictably oozing between boards in the dock before plopping unceremoniously into the black river Styx. Persephone was digging through one of her huge trunks, giggling at something unseen. RP watched, hoping the Boatman was done lecturing him. All he wanted to learn was the location of the nearest food.

"Just stay with me, I'm almost done." Charon poked RP with the staff, alerting him to the presence of a Binary Croteedian Baldoeanger slithering onto the dock from below.

"Aghhhh!" yelled RP, now fully attentive to his surroundings, leaping up and falling head first back into the stern of the skiff. His head hurt as badly as his stomach. The gnarly dude was pissing him off but he was too scared to admit it. RP still didn't get it. He'd never been on a planet or ship he could not escape simply by shifting his form. Why does Hell have no discernibly solid form he mused?

"That's because Hell is not a place," replied Charon. "This place exists even

outside of Astral levels one and two. It pops in and out of being so quickly that no one in or out of body-physical has the capacity to get it, get it?"

RP rubbed his sore head. Denial was morphing into acceptance. He was stuck here until it was over, whenever that was. Sitting up with his back against the stern RP wondered if perhaps there was some truth to the story line, I mean, why WAS he here? It dawned on him that he could get out of here and sell this stuff to…

"What was that?" yelled the big guy leaning precariously close to RP's nose.

Why don't I smell his breath, wondered RP? You'd think something that gross would have smelly breath but…

"Because I'm not alive. I'm not a living thing." The Boatman answered his thought.

"Let's get this over so that I can get you back to her Highness and the dog," continued Charon.

"Like I was saying, Proserpina grew up. Her story blossoms during Earth time 1930s with the rise of powerful men during the WWII era. Earth astronomers had already recognized Pluto and named it as such. This pretold a crisis of those powerful men losing power in order for karma with Pluto to be fulfilled.

"In astrology, Pluto always brings in a shift in power, or force. Remember that force is negative power enacted against free will while true power is a neutral

energy from the soul. In Earth time 2006, Pluto was demoted from a planet to a dwarf planet. Was that good or ill? We shall see what comes. They then gave Ceres equal status to Pluto. Ceres and Pluto shared the changes, the responsibilities equally. That is the future of Earth humanity, to one day share equally the Divine Feminine with the Divine Masculine."

"So," began a newly curious RP, "does that mean Persephone is not a victim? She's here for a good reason?"

"Now you understand," congratulated Charon. "Her three headed pup signifies the triune nature of Earth life...mind, body and spirit."

"Well, that's actually pretty cool," said RP. "I get that. So, in Roman mythology Pluto, kinda the king of the underworld, abducted Proserpina to marry him. This started the season of cold and dark upstairs. It actually addresses a marriage of energies, right? Pluto borrows power from higher up and sets it into the fabric of the shadow, the unconsciousness of human nature, representing the underworld, it's kinda weird that astronomers recognized Pluto around the same time those men came of power, then only to lose it. What was looking down on Earth from higher realms, then offer the atom bomb as a sacrifice to end the evil era."

RP felt proud of himself to ignore his body discomforts and rise to the occasion.

"But here's the thing," continued the Boatman. "Pluto energies beget tumultuous change and drama, clearing

the past for great change. To build anew. Happens second by second but you rarely see it happen. That's Ray One, by the way. The old forms, old beliefs and ways must die to present clear fresh ground for the new to grow. All this change can feel very personal but it's actually going on for everyone. Pluto is the volcano, the tsunami of lava, the giant iceberg hidden underneath the water's edge. It destroys and ends what needs to go quickly. Pluto is the verboten underbelly of Cerberus who hates being touched there. Pluto is forbidden territory coming to ruin your day because your day always has to end."

"Is that why beloved structures and old ways are dying out on Earth? I've never seen anything like it except on Xaaangir's third moon." mused RP.

"Yeah, that was actually an unscheduled unfortunate incident." sighed Charon.

"Pluto guarantees that what was unseen now shows up to get your attention in the most disruptive way possible. On a personal note, this shocks human's emotional Astral body out of complacency. It's going to hurt."

"Could you please get this dog thingy away from me?" RP inched closer to the edge of the skiff as Mr. Pup tried to cuddle RP. "Don't let it in this damn boat!" He begged.

Just then Persephone appeared seemingly out of this air to grab her

beloved's left head collar, yanking it away from the skiff.

"Awwww," she cooed. "Has him been bovering dem?"

Her Jasmine-scented hair wafting gracefully close to RP. He felt drunk and giddy around this goddess.

He smiled dreamily, watching her sit atop the giant dog, comforting and calming its three grinning heads. Three giant chew sticks appeared in her hands, tossing them expertly into three gaping mouths.

"You know what I miss down here?" she began. "I miss real light, you know, sunlight and all that. I miss lamb burgers and horse races and not having to grow up. This dependent feminine thingy traps females until we learn that we ARE the mystery, we ARE the silence within. Now that's powerful. I came here to grow up,

but also to demonstrate I can be strong while allowing the men to retain their own warrior strength. That's what's really going to come from all this, you know. We'll figure it out." She shifted her billowing white dress onto the back of the dog, appearing even more exquisite with every tiny movement. RP thought he was going to faint.

Facing RP she said "You might have noticed that lack of sparkle. The only light down in Hell comes from the thoughts of people who sent themselves here. I mean they did have some lovely thoughts and they did do some good up there. That's the tiny pieces of light here. It kind of glows in a dark way, right?"

RP noticed nothing except his unmentionable attraction to the cooing

vision sucking all the oxygen out of the room.

"Oxygen?" Persephone read his mind. "There's no oxygen here because you don't need it. I mean, you're in your Astral body so you don't need to breathe, right?" She slid off the back of her pup and approached the skiff.

"When my husband brought me here I thought I was alive in a physical body, but nope. It all goes back to my mother. I still like food and Perrier and chocolate espresso beans even though I know I don't need to eat, right?" Checking something in her pocket.

"Growing up major sucked. I didn't get to date a lot. I felt lonely. I did like that guy Sisyphus but he had that boulder issue, you know. That didn't go well. Then there was Achilles who had that weird thing with his heel. And Orpheus was gone a lot. Hercules was like a huge ego guy and Jason was obsessed with gold sheep. I don't know if any of them really liked me but the whole lot of them had huge emotional agendas."

Persephone visibly darkened, her beauty paled with some emotion known only in Hell. She shifted her gaze slightly, running her hand languidly through Cerberus' thick fur. When she finally looked up, a slight smile lightened the corners of her mouth, now ready to speak a truth unspoken and hidden until now.

"So, here's the deal with Mom" she began. "When I was called Kore, which means young girl, I could do no wrong. Zeus, my father was kind of absent but not unknown in my heart. I mean, he had a lot going on being head god and all. My mom, Demeter, loved nature as did I. Her job was to guard and honor the harvests. That was way cool for me because I got to see how it all works. As long as I was Kore, everything went as we planned. Although lots of the gods wanted to hang with me, no one dared bother me due to Dad's influence and sharp eye over my well being."

RP was hungry, again, this story wasn't helping and his stomach growled so loudly that Cerberus growled right back, at least the middle head did.

"OMG, you think you need food!" the goddess giggled at him. "I'm so sorry, I forgot your bodies are half in and half out. Here! Take this." she handed RP a huge bagel slathered in cream cheese and loaded with lox and capers.

"How'd she do that?" he mused, grabbing it before her dog lunged.

With RP gnashing contentedly on the bagel, Persephone continued her tale.

"Like I was saying, Dad had everything handled until that stuff with Pluto started. He can be a real ass. Well, both of them can actually. They never got along anyway and Mom thought Pluto was just gross. That didn't help because I adore his weirdo self. I know what you're thinking. Oh! Poor Persephone, she's rebelling and going with that awful man!

Everyone says it. Where they have it wrong in the story books is believing that Pluto saw me picking flowers in that meadow and just grabbed me, taking me down into Hell. Really?! I'd never let anyone do that. I'm not an idiot, you know. Why do they always need a female victim to be rescued? He was the craziest, most exciting thing I'd ever seen. Nobody let me date and I was bored stiff, so Pluto was my answer to getting outta town, right? Okay, maybe that gossip's a little true."

Persephone sighed and looked out over the Styx. RP had finished his gnosh and was picking his teeth with something resembling a fish bone. Cerberus' three heads were asleep, huge front paws relaxing on the skiff's edge. The Boatman sighed. He'd seen this play out before, some half this or that winding up wallowing around in Hell, confused and miserable. Maybe not just yet. But this little alien was different, he mused. What

was it? He seemed really intelligent but irritable as all get out.

"What?" voiced the goddess, "I heard that. What do you think we should do with him?" she concluded.

"With me?" began RP, "Why do you need to do anything with me?! Just get me out of here!" He jumped up, banging his leg on the edge of the slimy dock.

Three heads snorted, looking up at their lady for what to do next. The three heads were actually one thought process divided into three available outcomes. It's not written anywhere, so there you go.

Cerberus and Persephone stopped and looked at RP. The drab light of Hell now shimmered and wobbled as if decaying into the Styx. Was the whole thing falling apart, leaving RP stranded in this Astral

manifestation? He looked at his hands and feet wobbling in and out of form. Charon's voice sounded distant and faint.

"Just get back in the boat," he encouraged.

"Not if you're taking me farther into Hell," cried RP. He was really scared now, embarrassed that they saw this part of him. RP crawled shakily into the skiff seating himself on the slimy bench. He felt a bit more solid but that was about to change dramatically. At least the dog thingy wasn't near. Persephone smiled at RP and turned around to leave.

"Come on Bee Bee," she cooed. Jasmine wafted over the dock, perfuming the air. He wondered if the Ferryman smelled it. Not that it mattered.

"What DOES matter here?" he began to relax. In fact, was he too relaxed?

"Am I drugged or something?" His words sounded syrupy and distant. The skiff rocked a bit as it floated silently back up the River Styx. RP's body felt unfamiliar. He could barely make out the edges of anything. Something was happening and he didn't know what.

"If I were on Noxab's third moon in Lerlia's Luxury House I'd actually enjoy sitting in the Neural Mist Pool with a glass of Borzab Beer. But I'm here, at least I think I'm here." But which here was it?

Brilliant light scorched the verdant landscape. The vast desert of southern Iraq rolled out from his ship as far as he could see. Miles and miles of nothing welcomed and awakened the traveller,

eyes adjusting and senses balancing in the dry air.

"Where am I?" he stood, scanning the landscape for a familiar landmark. The last thing he remembered before Hell was meeting with the Gnomes on Dagrett. Those six moons were so much fun. The Gnomes had met him there, handed him the glyphs, but then what?

"Damnit to hell!" RP climbed the ladder back into his ship. The alien bugs were swimming in his cup of Zakko Blue, drunk and apparently thrilled to be out of the drawer. RP watched them in his distracted state, unsure of where he was and what he was required to do.

His old steampunk ship floated a couple feet off the ground.

"Good! That's normal" he sighed in relief. "I have no idea what happened or if I dreamed all that." He looked at his clothes, slightly rumpled and too odiferous for even his taste.

"Why do I stink?" RP ran his hand through his hair then down the side of his pants. A scant aura of blackish goo clung loosely from his clothes. The warm desert of southern Iraq folded out before him like a welcome mat.

"Ok, well, I guess I was really there. But if I was in my Astral body, why do I stink like my physical body was there too?"

RP sat down and scanned the landscape. No one and nothing moved in the heat. He'd always liked this part of the world and recalled directing his ship to the edge

of nowhere before falling into this adventure.

"Oh, that's it." He stood and looked back at his ship. "Must have gotten red-zapped while relaxing on the blue moon."

"How long was I there, for god sake?! Maybe Zoli's right about me needing a couple months in that recovery center."

But what RP needed was a shower. He wandered over to his ship to rinse off with the Leaubeau sprayer projecting out of his self care pod.

"Now I feel more me." Looking out the side window, RP realized where he was and where he was supposed to be in ten minutes.

"Oh shit!" he jumped up, "Montana! I was supposed to meet Zoli up at the High

Country with the Gnome Glyphs. Craps, crap, crap!" The voyage into Hell now took backseat to his best buddy. He'd have some splainin' to do for sure.

"Ok, focus, focus." RP dug through his closet for the shimmery bag of glyphs the Gnostic Gnomes charged him with handing over to Z.

"Where's the damn thing?" RP trashed the pod, tossing anything and everything onto the shiny floor. A tiny creature skidded to a stop, followed by a dozen or more alien bugs multiplying as they crawled.

"She's gonna kill me." He quit digging and leaned back against the edge of the ship. Now what, he mused. He couldn't have left them anywhere else because he hadn't been anywhere else, had he? What part of him visited Hell and what part unmanifested? Wandering over to the sleep couch, he plopped his exhausted body onto the purple fur and closed his eyes.

"Just for a minute," he promised no one. The bugs stopped crawling and watched RP, hoping to catch a meal before morphing into their new bodies. But nothing. RP was crashed.

Minutes rolled into hours. The crisp night air pressed a welcome breeze through the open door. Something yipped far off in the desert, but RP was deep in his needed rest to notice.

BOOM! The cracking thunder shook him off the couch, tossing him onto the floor. Daylight broke open his eyes and shocked his memory enough to stand and look out the window. A tendril of black smoke wafted miles away. BOOM! Again, RP grabbed the edge of the couch to steady himself. "Okay, that smoke show is minutes and clicks from me."

"Damnit to hell, Iraq. How could I forget?" A third explosion, this one closer, encouraged him to quit dilly dallying and get out of dodge.

"Yeah, the old west, that's what this is." More booms and the clipping of a chopper met him as he hustled over to the controls.

"I know I'm not 3D visible but that sounds like a Huey or maybe a Chinook? No, it's

an Apache," he recalled Thom schooling him on Iraq. "Where are my shoes?"

BOOM! "No time. That sounded close. Those RPGs go boom around 11,000 to 12,000 yards. That detonation signature is too much for me to deal with right now."

RP focused and imagined his ship hugging the snowy cliffs of Montana. No boom booms there. Closing his eyes, RP pressed his thoughts through the looking glass of his mind.

"All aboard!" he giggled. The momentary distraction of space shifting felt damn good. There it was, Mount Jumbo crowning Missoula. "But where's the damn airport?"

The thought of it manifested him right to it. The roof was, well, new. Had they redone the airport since he was last here pre pandemic? Looks like it. RP slid off the black fur console seat and peered out over the city. The High Country was a bit to the northeast from here so he could make it in a few seconds. But what about Hell? Did that really happen? Could he have lost the Glyphs during a dematerialized manifest?

Travelers in jeans and hoodies exited cars and trucks, toiling mightily with their carry-ons and large suitcases bound for somewhere else. RP watched and wondered. The suitcase bearers, gobbled up by the new building seemed to shake loose a memory. But what was it?

RP watched some alien girls sunning themselves on Pleiadian elevated deck chairs, unseen by travelers or anyone human. This roof was getting interesting.

"Oh! That's it!" he turned and tripped over the pile of tossed everything. "The Glyphs are in the stasis chamber. I encoded them there before playing on that moon."

RP kicked the drawer contents out of the way and hurried over to the floating shimmery globe bouncing elegantly on top of the elevating disc. He loved how that worked because it did. No G force shift affected it so anything he placed in the 2x2 foot globe was safe. He could even raise the frequency to invisible. The setting for remote manifestation had been set days ago by a then sober RP. He marveled at succeeding to reappear it exactly when needed. How it knew was always mysterious. Its creator was long gone so users trusted Gratitude

frequency, allowing it to read the temporal future and, well, work.

New sounds reached his ears as somebody's dog barked joyously from the pick up bed as his returned person set down his backpack to scrunch some doggie ears. A quick honk, the polite Montana, excuse me but get the F out of the way, sound rushed the morning unaware of two small alien ships populating the roof above. And something smelled good. Coffee and bear claw scents wafted up from the open slider alongside the entrance to the airport. But none of this mattered to RP whose joyous relief noticed only the floating globe.

"Now, how do I get these things outta here without activating the dematerializing trigger?" RP stood a foot away, hands out as if magicking it to behave. A soft buzzing reminded him that it was pre set and he didn't have to DO anything except feel honest gratitude. Its creator knew that love is the glue holding together all worlds, so he programmed the thing to respond to real living gratitude, not a fakery glamour. It could tell the difference because you can't fake truth in the presence of Truth.

RP smiled, opening his heart and mind to the universal frequency of gratitude and true love. It felt good after relinquishing his heart to that lower chakra panic of survival in Hell. Nope, done with that.

The shimmery globe emitted a popping sound that RP still swears was a

frequency of joy. A small lavender bag tied loosely at the top with a gold strand plopped unceremoniously onto the floor.

"Should I pick it up?" he hesitated. "I've only used this thing twice and the other time it dematerialize the box when I touched it."

The little bag said nothing, it rested on the floor as though testing RP to do something, but what?

"Well it makes sense that I should continue projecting the gratitude frequency into my hands as I pick it up, right? I mean, it's been soaking up the Truth frequency and I don't wanna shock it into disappearing. The Gnomes would chase me down for an eternity if I screw this up."

Lucky for him, love is never far from a loving heart, and RP had a loving heart. Bending down he lovingly lifted the bag and held it in two hands.

"Nothing weird here," he tested. "Maybe I passed the test."

A screechy giggle broke through the love, forcing RP to again look at the alien reveller gals now peering over the edge of the roof at some poor fool whose suitcase contents were splattered on the sidewalk.

An Alaska Air plane lifted off its scheduled 05:59 flight to Seattle. The morning felt kinda normal, save the aliens on the roof.

RP returned his gaze to the lavender bag in his hands. Walking over the strewn mess on the floor he gently replaced the bag in the drawer and sighed. Now, he could head up the High Country.

"I wonder if Zoli has intuited what I'm gonna give her?" He focused now on the aerial controls, closing his eyes and imagining the location. The Montana morning did not disappoint. The view from his window reminded him why Zoli and Thom moved here from Olympia a while back. Hopefully, he could add to that joy by delivering the Glyphs. The Gnostic Gnomes swore that they could "change the world." Maybe just the world of the few people they were created to help. Gnomes spent too much time chilling out and smoking weed for him to believe all they said was true. At least that was his own experience with them.

He felt good now. The Hell thingy was a distant memory. Food was available and all way right with the world.

COMING SOON, RP AND THE GNOSTIC GNOME GLYPHS by Zoli and illustrated by Saurana.

I agreed to forget, to not know, to come into an Earth body for as long as it took because time is forever and it matters not how long it takes.

The hand stops and invites, a universal symbol of communication sans words. This hand speaks with Pluto, Aries, and the Moon. It volumizes excess with the fire of life, tinged with the lunar illusion that nothing matters or it all does.

Sleep Until You Dream

I've been reading up on sleep; who and how we have slept in the past. Did you know that up until the 1950s it was the norm to sleep with others in a non sexual way?

Let me clarify! Up until the mid-19th century communal sleeping was the norm. Travelers usually shared a bed with companions or even folks they did not know. Beds were a commodity and the rule was that you hoped your bed partner didn't stink, fart, snore, or move around much.

Communal sleeping was the norm. Can you imagine today, heading to the B&B to share the bed with total strangers?

In the early 1900s, this sleeping norm began to shift. Why? Industry. Beds were more common.

Wealth began distributing more into the middle class, allowing personal freedoms to replace lack thereof.

I think we are so forward looking that we often pooh-pooh the behaviors of the past, seeing them as just dumb. But are we really more evolved because we sleep, or eat differently?

I giggle at myself considering what I'll think of me in a decade. Will I see my current behavior as silly? Maybe I'll be more evolved, but certainly I'll be older. What do you think?

WAKEY WAKEY

Do you ever feel you just got something that had been bugging you for too long? Why does that happen? Do we get what is intended for us, kind of like a billboard all lit up displaying that answer?

How do we choose the right stuff from that eternal void of endless possibilities?

The creativity of synchronicity partnered with the vast pool of potential choices is the stuff of dreams. But why choose? Isn't everything happening as it is supposed to? Of course not. Not everything happens for a reason because we are here to consciously make reason out of chaos. What happens if no choice is made, no illuminated answers help us choose?

Some of us cruise through life unawares. Whatever happens, happens. Tweedle Dum and Tweedle Dee, life is just as it should be. What happens, really? The safeguard set into motion before birth are the woo-woo charts; the numerology, astrology, physical body charts, and all the reality-discerning boundaries acting like pathways carrying the unconscious traveler to predestined outcomes. That's auto pilot.

We play out the archetypal predestined roles assigned by our soul. What? Can't we change that? Of course, we do when we say "Wait a minute, what do I want?" When we awaken and become curious about the reasons we are here anyway, focusing finally on those skills specific to navigating this earthly realm. That's the awakening enacted.

The charts still continue, but awareness of potential patterns and discerning who we are with them changes everything. Magnificent energy fields present as deep emotion. Feelings color the stark landscape with tender offerings to the soul. It doesn't just happen.

Awareness is the grace falling into open hands praying for that feeling of love. Love is always the answer. What do we have to do to enact that loving awareness, that precious curiosity ever-present in the wings as we act out on the stage of life?

What do we need to change, how should we act and with whom?

All this changes when the fog lifts and the clarion call from the soul births enlightenment into the vessel of the personality.

The soul reaches and teaches, aligning self with self. It is a Master on its own plane and we access it through love. Why is it true that love is all there is? Tell me what you feel. Love is who you are, in this reality and all others. Go in peace.

TEMET NOSCE: KNOW THYSELF

Temet nosce, know thyself, was a much repeated lesson from my mom to my adolescent personality. I often thank her spirit for the wisdom offered and the ongoing lesson of discernment.

The lifelong path of becoming authentic engages the discomfort of self discovery as we bump into emotion sheltering fear.

Who would we be if we were truly authentic, devoid of projection and pretense, in continual alignment with the soul?

We come into physical bodies to experience physical things. These experiences engage emotional reactions. Our pre-birth agreements allow these experiences. The lesson offered is the experience of emotion rather than the specific event. The emotions are those gems in the crown of the Divine which elevate drama to detachment.

Life experiences appear to us as pleasant or painful. The emotions overrule clarity as pain overrules detachment. How often

do we choose detachment from pleasure? Is this not the passion of addiction, to increase pleasure and block pain?

The World Teacher, Maitreya, states "The greatest drug is detachment." Pain challenges that.

The emotion of fear holds hands with pain. The physical body fears its demise. When we hurt, we fight the pain and curse the body. We separate ourselves from this most precious gift of life on Earth because

> The spirit works through us in a different way. Once we do fifty one percent of the work, Spirit comes in and adds to that. That's my theory.

we are not feeling pleasure. This is our addiction.

I am writing and pondering this because of a recent physical distress. A histamine increase within my ears presented as a painful pressure and reduction of hearing from blocked eustachian tubes and inner ear imbalance.

I observed my emotional body tempting me with dramatic fear, "Maybe I am losing my hearing. Sounds are distorted and I feel light-headed. I'm having

trouble socializing due to this blocked hearing."

These fears badgered my consciousness as I lay in bed seeking sleep. I felt challenged to remain mentally focused as my gut rumbled with irrational fear. Self-talk, prayer and binaural beat auditory meditations seemed to calm the emotions. I felt it was a test to see if I could remain focused, right?

I awakened the next morning to the still plugged ears, grateful for the prescribed homeopathics and meds on board. I sleepily wandered into the bathroom and looked out the huge window with a view of the south side of our mountain. What was that? A large bird slowly walked around a tree grove fifty yards away. I could not discern the color but noticed a large beak and its size, certainly not a songbird. Was it one of our wild turkeys? Not the right color and that beak was too predatory. Maybe a raven but still much larger. I smiled as I observed it circumvent the grove and languidly wander up the mountain, not a care in the world.

Birds are special to my soul. I have five winged creatures in my personal medicine chart. Although I feel no

I then read my morning messages from The Catholic Company's Morning Offering: "Jesus said to Nicodemus 'You must be born from above, the wind blows where it wills and you can hear the sound it makes but you do not know where it comes from or to where it goes. So it is with everyone who is born of the Spirit.' (Jonn 3:7) The Holy Spirit blows where it wills." (John 3:8)

These two morning gifts affirmed my current lesson of trusting that God's Will is all that is. If I can release my fearful emotions unto the wind of Spirit, that is comfort. The test continues as I ponder my pre-birth set up to resolve this release of desolation into consolation.

particular alignment with them, winged creatures appear to follow me, an oxymoron confounding my feeble personality.

But this morning as my coffee and I rested next to the living room window, a huge bird winged gracefully down the gulch, causing me to choke a bit in surprise. Ah! A red tailed hawk! That's who it was on the hill.

Hawk medicine offers opportunity to consider that Great Spirit's home is the grand Beyond. It offers that we consider grace in simplicity and reverence when presented with earthly woes. Hawk is Mercury, the mythological messenger of the gods bringing words of the Divine Unknown into mundane reality.

Perhaps the acceptance of this pre-birth set up can offer compassion of self and detachment. That said, not all experiences are exact pre-birth set ups. As we evolve mentally and spiritually the addiction to emotion dissolves gracefully

into detached observation. Certainly the karmic lessons evolve as we do, some in pain and even more in joy. We have more good karma than bad, but attach in reticence to the lack of pleasure.

Emotional reactions remove us from the precious present. The temptation is to wallow in memories and probable unpleasant futures. It is suggested that the brain/mind cannot tell the difference between past and future. Is it because these temporal constructs exist only as tools? Detachment from emotional reaction comes when we choose to focus attention at the Ajna center, the sixth chakra in between the eyebrows. This releases neurochemicals which calm the emotions and return attention to the present experience.

Fears do not live in the heart or the head. They reside within the lower chakras, sticking to the third one below the heart. This is the epicenter of emotional reactivity. No circumstance or activity causes emotion, as the reactivity to those effects of life are self generated and attach fully to memories. The world is neutral while our emotions color circumstance and experience.

We become attenuated to the leisurely acceptance that emotions are to be expressed at any cost. Feeling emotions and expressing them to others can result in destruction or reconstruction of relationships. Unpleasant feelings do not always require the involvement of others, as they have their own demons to fight.

Demons? Unpleasantries can feel like that. What are the consequences of overt emotional behavior as opposed to detached observation of feelings? Feeling angry is one thing but expressing anger can be, well, consequential. There is a fine line between expressing anger appropriately and blowing steam as though we deserve the outburst, damn the consequences. But I digress. Do these physical circumstances set the stage to feel emotion? They appear to do just that. Chinese medicine councils balance by not seeking too much pleasure or happiness. It councils that detached observation honors the extremes by allowing in a bit of both poles.

Evolving societal norms of compassion for self and others lifts us out of emotional turmoil into that calm perception of acceptance.

Acceptance of what exactly? That we are incarnated souls experiencing life on Earth, brazenly confronting our fears, our lives and our inner selves. That is…

hard to do, but Earth school appears to offer these lessons while connection with Divine Source is the calming panacea to emotional turmoil. The authentic self waits in the wings, whispering cues and comfort on the stage of life. When loving compassion replaces fear and reaction, great patience and reticence of behavior brushes wings with the Holy Spirit, that mysterious spirit from the beyond. Go in peace!

MENTAL ILLNESS AND DENSITIES

The mind and emotions become enmeshed within the constructs of conflicting densities. These densities are conflictual in their essence because their frequencies live on different levels. As the higher realms demonstrate in levels, so do densities. These are not dimensions but personal realities which answers the question of why the mentally distressed are isolated from the greater reality we share.

I awakened at 02:00, unable to sleep due to disturbing impressions representing

fears we all share. The human fear of isolated abandonment in times of need is acutely entrenched in the landscape of nightmares and disturbances while awake. These disturbances are emotions habituating specific densities connected to the lower Astral realms. I myself could not restfully sleep because some imprint was poking at the outer realms of my consciousness, begging entry. The imprint was this image that mental and emotional disturbances are specific densities. If this is so, we titrate drugs and substances both recreationally and medically to meld the emotional body

with desired densities for healing or detriment.

We are a drugged society addicted to densities supporting neurotransmitters which engage these densities. If we view both the "high" and the "balancing" aspects as densities rather than 3D energies, perhaps the ideation of imbalances can be recalibrated by addressing the density rather than only the manifested emotions.

Again the question of why humans enter this reality desiring to drug themselves out of it addresses the enticement of these densities. Perhaps densities are emotional archetypes programmed into the experience of life on earth. Or perhaps they are self created anomalies generated by attachments to emotions. The feeling nature begs solace as well as resolution of conflicts, whether self generated or presented from external stimuli. The ability to detach from the emotional component of a density appears to relegate imbalanced emotions to the mental realm. However, mental attachments (Illusions) are also density specific. The emotional attachments (Glamours) similarly stick to human experience and our discomforting pressure from within to seek solace.

The hardened stubbornness of mental illness and addiction insist upon remaining immune to balance, whatever that looks like. The addiction may be the emotional body grounding itself firmly within the cage of a density. In other words, an emotional density appears to block light from the mind and the Source from realigning the emotional body with the mental body. The fights observed between these two bodies present in all addictive persons. The mental illnesses also appear to be stuck in between mental and emotional comfort and resolution of conflicting states.

Frequencies and fields are universal while densities are personal and experienced with the flavors of frequencies. Dimensions, like fields, are universal. Densities exist within dimensions and are experienced personally with awareness of their universality. The incoming fifth dimension engages its non linearality and expansiveness while one remains, living life, in the third dimensional world. The dynamics of higher consciousness allow the experiencing of fifth dimensional

abilities while the individual remains engaged with the normal world. Emotional and mental densities then express as "spiritual" experiences with affects of connection to the shared reality of 3D, stimulating grace and balance between the emotional and mental bodies.

Questions:

Is addiction to a substance actually addiction to the density?

Is addiction to any substance or behavior actually only one density? Is that why we label all these behaviors "addictions"?

At what point does the emotional body engage the mental body with density conflict? Is this the moment when we realize there is a conflict, meaning the defining behavior is consciously recognizable?

Theories anyone? *Nullum Bonum Inpunitum*

GARGOYLES

You thought I forgot, didn't you? You wanted to know why gargoyles smell, and all that. I didn't forget, I was only trying to find the right words to explain it to you. You know how a smell invokes emotions and memory? Cut grass in summertime coupled with the grind of the lawn mower...the smell of cookies baking and the low hum of the convection oven, those images and scents work together to create scenes.

But what about the five inner senses, how do they work? The inner sight, hearing, smell, taste and inner touch act together and a bit faster. Maybe because we don't have to connect them immediately to the physical world. That sounds confusing, I hear you. Let me explain. The inner senses attend to the third eye and its sensory ability to tune into the non physical aspects of the physical. You do this all the time but it's more autonomic than general.

Well, I've confused you again. Hmmm. How about this...we've all experienced "knowing" who was on the phone or being aware something was going to happen before it shows up literally. Right? Okay, we're on the same page now. You know and feel these non physical experiences with your non physical senses. Bingo! You feel the physical world through the physical senses and the unseen world with your "unseen" senses. Do it all the time without even thinking about it. But those non physical senses are the ones

that connect with the unseens, the Devic beings and the like.

But digress, I do that a lot, you say. Do gargoyles smell? Oh, come on Zoli, what'd you put in your orange juice? No really, they smell kind of musky but not in a bad way, not sour, just like an old sweater. I never smell gnomes or dwarfs, but I can identify a gargoyle smell from that of a troll. Trolls smell like an opened box of stuff from the woods, multi scented actually. There is a grassy, mossy smell, a sour violet and something like a dog's paw. Do they all smell the same? Dunno. The ones I know smell like that.

What about faeries? Glad you asked. They smell like wind chimes sound. There it is again, you guys, the scent and auditory thingies mesh into one communication. I wish I understood it more but hope you have some insight to share.

I'm not unaware how bizarre and fantastical this sounds. I myself am challenged with actualizing truth from fantasy when dancing with the gods of lower realms. There's so much out there, so many frequencies, beings, ways of perceiving. I sit on the edge of sanity at times. Coffee helps. Adderall did not. Can't do weed because it makes me fat,

lazy and hiding in the closet in a paranoid funk. I'm telling you this because you sometimes feel a tad iffy yourself. Guess what? That's normal. Whew.

When we access other worlds, other frequencies, we have to let go of the good old normal reality we share. But how often do you sneak a peek at other folks' thoughts in the woo woo department? Other folks feel as crazy as you do at times.

But this is how we adjust. We access, adjust, then take a break from it and surf the net or something to distract and allow all that inner goo to solidify into a newer neural network capable of accessing

higher frequencies and weirder beings. Welcome to Zoli land.

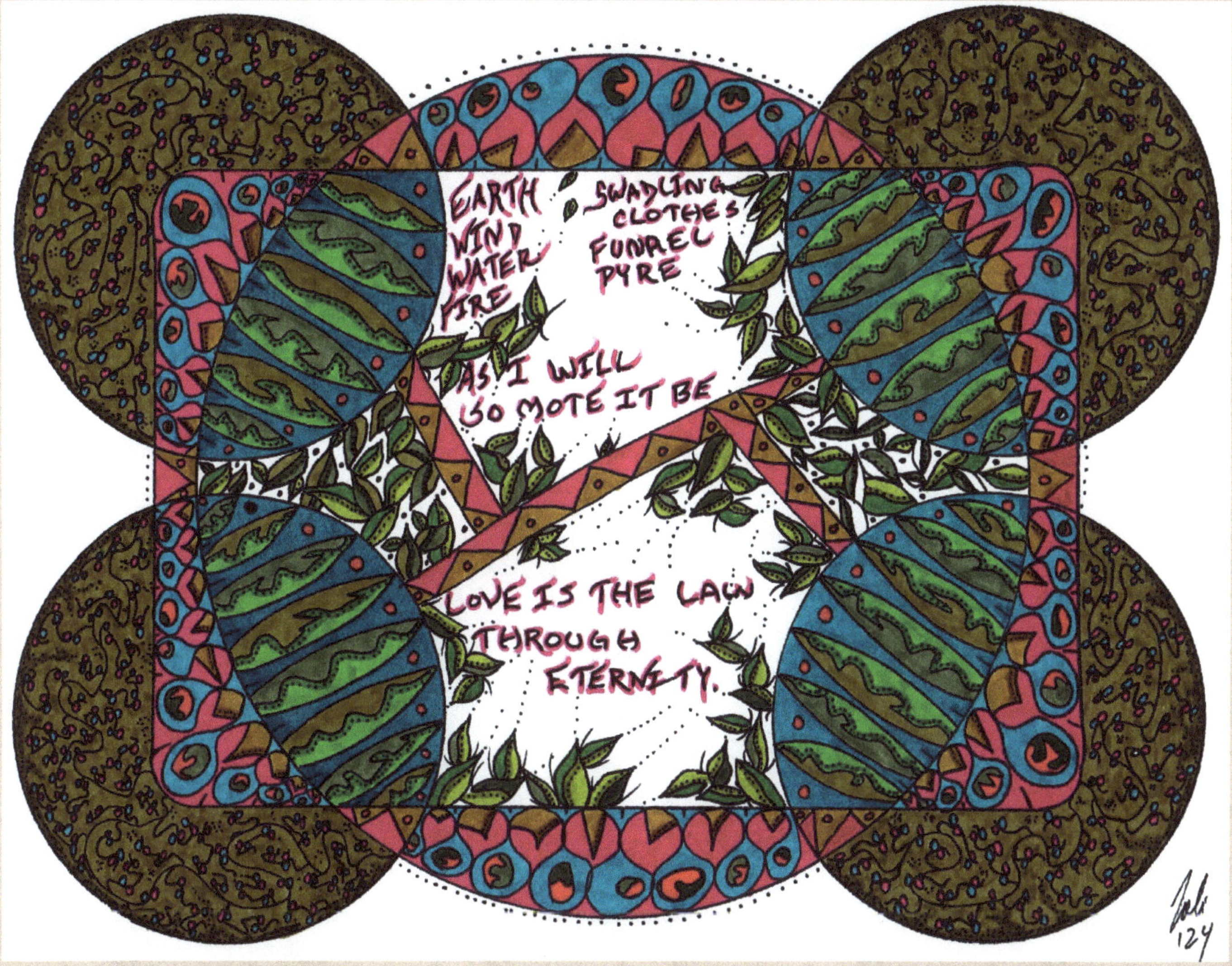

Earth Wind Water Fire, swaddling clothes, funeral pyre. As I Will, so mote it be. Love is the law through eternity. The elements offer interaction with themselves and others in form. The material world cycles as all things have a beginning, middle and end. The Will powers evolution with desire and intent. Love is all there is, everywhere.

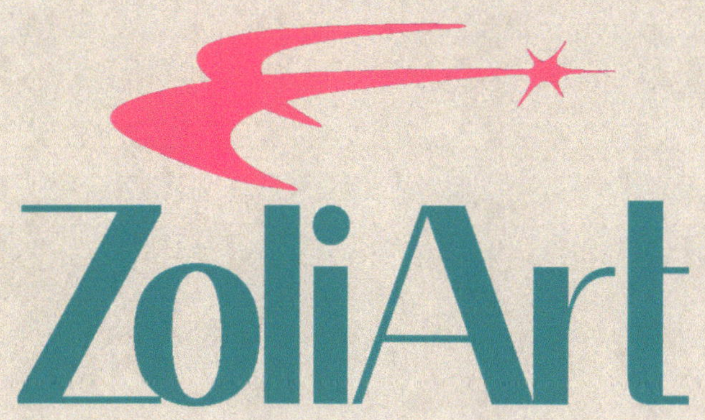

What do you read in your local morning news?

I awakened to a Montana-ish article about some pack mules from the Ranger District hauling 1,000 pounds of explosives to evict the archaic dam hugging the corner of the Rattlesnake Wilderness near Missoula.

Dynamite is a legal use item in the Montana wilderness, fancy that. But understand that the Montana wilderness can be your neighborhood if you live remote. Just saying, Tannerite is loud at 2 a.m.

The article continues to report that Trout Unlimited worked with the Forest Service commissioned to deconstruct ten old dams beneath these lofty peaks.

It was the image of the local pack mules servicing the steep mountain trails that stuck with me. Montana bleeds archaic into modern. We unabashedly slather methods and materials all over modern challenges as if no time had passed at all.

MONTANA MADNESS

Fascination with the TV series Yellowstone, filmed down the Bitterroot Valley from here paints a Montana landscape arguing with itself as opposed to wandering delightfully through West Yellowstone park proper. What's a girl to do?

Last week I chatted with a good gal friend from the citified East Coast, complaining that I don't shop downtown Missoula because my big-ass F-150 Raptor refuses to hug those teensy parking spots. Her solution was a reasonable yet misunderstood solution that "Why don't I instead take my car?"

And what car is that? Our driveway up here at Dragon Crest Ranch sports said

Raptor, a work truck 350 with over 100,000 miles a new diesel 350, a snowmobile perched on a trailer, three quads, a side by side, a Rokon off road motorbike, the boneyard of someday-we-will-need-these parts and tools, a water trailer for forestry, and stuff. But all the stuff and vehicles allow one to prep their way through 27 degree below winters and smoky summers. Montana is an acquired taste similar to happily deluded fools believing they can make it in Alaska because they bought some remote parcel off the grid.

Let's see what else is on today's local news that I can relate to your curious self!

Montana argues it is a fiercely Libertarian state, so lots of letters to the editor on who has what right, democracy vs. autocracy flavor. Last night a subadult female (translates as young and dumb) black bear attacked a kiddo in his tent.

A fed bear is a dead bear, we say. The now shot bear surely smelled food. The kid is okay, this time.

The Miller Creek (pronounced locally as Crik) fire is mostly contained and the fire danger on Lolo Peak just south of Missoula, is contained. Mercifully, summer fire season has produced few fires and less smoke, which was awesome when our seven year old grandson visited and spent a week literally outside collecting wild turkey feathers and a few antler sheds.

Our water levels are way down, global drought and all. Today's paper says the Clark Fork near Missoula historically pumps at 1,470 feet per second but today is at 747. The Blackfoot River near Bonner isn't any better at 422 cfps when it wants to be 815.

MONTANA MADNESS

For lack of culturally appropriate intel, the paper ran an article from Rome on Dolce and Gabbana dog perfume, $108 for 3.4 ounces. Guess you'd have to order that as our local stores may miss the mark. And just what do we sport here for local stores? Target, Dillard's, Cabela's, two Walmarts, Lowe's, Home Depot, lots of hardware and sport and food stores including our new Shields. We do have a mall, a mall-ette rather. Two hoity French restaurants, Applebee's, Cracker Barrel, seven local diners like Rubys, and a plethora of nail salons, little casinos, a pot

store and a booze store every other corner. What's a girl to do?

The local paper both ignores and toots our horn on the quality of life here. Montana is a rural state, a poor state at that. I was curious as to how many of our roads are paved. A web site from Billings claims we have 73,571 miles of public roads in the state, with 73,000 of those public roads paved. Doesn't look like that once you get out of the cities! But I guess that's fortunate if you want to drive across Montana which takes about 21 hours. Not by pack mules...

Sometimes when people die, they do not know they're dead. I've had a lot of experiences with that when somebody dies suddenly, like in a car wreck.

After I had been living on my the farm for about a year, I went into town and heard that there was this boy that was killed on the highway near me.

The road there can be a bit tricky, it's only a narrow two-lane country road in that spot of Hwy 99 SE. The boy in question was headed to his prom in Tenino when he ran off the road, and ended upside

down on the hill. And I thought, oh, boy. I hope he doesn't wander down the hill to the house and end up here.

Sure as shit, when I was sitting in my office, in the back of the house, I looked up only to see him standing there. He was covered in blood. It scared the hell out of me. Three dead young boys were with him. I'll never forget this. They were close to his age and all laughing with him about crashing his car. It was such a visual.

People that die in crisis, can wander around the Earth for a very long time.

And why is that? Well, if people are not spiritual or do not consider when they are alive what is going to happen when they're on the other side, they might get stuck. No one knows for sure, but you need to get into the feeling and being forewarned is forearmed.

Being prepared, that's what I also write about in *Law Enforcement and the Paranormal.* Don't let something just happen when you're rolling on a call. Think beforehand about what you're going to do. So, that's why we train and the statement in gun training is that in a crisis, you'll do what you're trained to do. So, it's important, and all the religions talk about that, but they put the big prayer and guilt thing on it, which they shouldn't.

Think about the other world. Consider that you're not here forever and consider where you will go and what will happen. I think the major religions don't always address that in a proper way because there's a feeling attached to it. When you die in a crisis, so to speak, you're immediately in the etheric or astral realm. And the etheric realm is part of the physical world. That's where the invisible lives. Even though you can't see it with the physical senses, you can see it with the inner psychic senses.

So, when somebody dies, especially in a crisis or if they're sick and they die and they they're afraid of going over to the other side, they may just hang out in aunt Elizabeth's living room for years trying to get their attention. Anything you can imagine happens. But part of the problem with the crisis deaths, is that the minute they die it is a shock.

If you die before the time that you were destined to die, you will stay connected to the Earth. It's just a weird thing. It's not a punishment, but we have to finish our days. That is why the nursing homes are so filled with people, conscious, unconscious, sick, that sort of thing.

They're waiting out until their time comes. So, what happens if you die and it's a normal death? Well, you will go through what the Buddhist called the Bardo.

The Bardo is the cycle where you meet your fears, it's very complicated, and I don't want to get into it because I'm going to mess it up because I'm not Buddhist. But you meet yourself, all the people that you've been in this life, all the personalities, everything about you. And how does that happen if you've lived a

had. All their cats will be there when they die.

God loves you that much to make that happen. Is it an illusion? Yeah. It is. And how long does that go on? I don't know. It can go on for days, weeks, months, years. But at some point, we wake up on the other side or we just run out of given time to where we move into the next phase.

We can train ourselves not to get stuck when we die. And it happens a lot. Absolutely. You do it before you die, before you get in the accident by saying if that happens to me, I invoke help from

hundred years in a few seconds? There's no time on the other side.

Everything happens at once, and it's more of an intensity of a feeling. And it just happens. It's not connected to the Earth plane. And probably people you knew before will show up and help you. Or if those people are moved on, or if they don't want to do it, maybe they didn't like you that much, then somebody that you imagine them to be will show up. A spirit will take their form, and that happens a lot. If people think they're going to die, they're going to meet all their cats they've

what I believe in. Jesus, Buddha, Christ, Moses, I don't know. Santa Claus. Whatever you believe in, that that will show up to help carry you over. Then, if you have an accident and you kill your physical body, you will know how to lift your thoughts and not get stuck in the shock.

You see what I'm saying? You can plan that, and that does need to be planned. We need to say I believe in Christ. I believe in the Buddha, or whatever it is you believe. Or simply repeat when I die, I believe that I will see the light and I will be carried into bliss. And that's pretty much what will happen. So, your belief is your will. That is your willpower, and you are shooting your will into what God's big petri dish wants to grow for you.

You have that ability, and you really should do that. You have the right to do that. And I try not to tell people what you should do or what you have to do. But in order for that to happen, you have to be prepared.

LAUNDRY ROOM WARRIOR

"So, I'm going to go now if you don't need me," said the detached voice. I pulled my head out of the dryer, unceremoniously dumping the clean clothes on the floor before looking up to see which entity was nudging me to respond.

A seven-foot warrior stood in complete kit, gloved hand on the pistol grip of his M4 rifle, pant legs in camouflage bulging with filled mags and God knows what else, sunglasses shading his eyes and a night vision contraption raising from his helmet like a vulture in flight.

"Ow!" I stood up, bonking my head on the dryer door. "Yeah, you can go. Thanks for the help." I faced a slowly dematerializing etheric being whom I swear grinned at me before poofing out of the room.

Welcome to Zoliland. These beings patrol my property, ride in the passenger seat of my F150 Raptor as I drive, their left arm resting on the M4 on the console. I live this like it's normal. Why are they here and am I bat shit crazy? Is my over active imagination making this up? I've written previously about the difference between scripting a visualization and the real deal when these guys present in etheric form, but I know you forgot so here goes.

If I were to imagine a being or a scene, there is a picture in my head of how it progresses. It's very mental. But when an etheric being manifests, it's game on. I can't tell what comes next because it's not mine. It's like a living person is doing the acting and it's not seen in my head but through my eyes. Physical eyes? Kind of.

Let me explain. The physical eyes and ears allow the INNER senses of sight and sound to activate. Usually. A blind person can certainly etherically communicate, as can someone without physical hearing. But it differs because it is neither imagined nor acted out in the exact same way. When a sighted person sees an etheric bring he uses the customary sense to attend to that. It's like a dual experience. I don't physically hear the warrior speak but I KNOW it rather than hear it. I see him but it is not with physical eyes.

I'm kind of mucking this up because it's hard to explain. Maybe one of you all can do a better job than me. Which brings me to my fave subject which is Everyone Can Do This but has had the inner psychism

squelched by the necessity of attending to the much needed five physical senses. True dat. So, take a shot at explaining this phenomena better than I, thank you.

You're wondering why the Tier One Operator shows up and hangs with me. Why not an artist or a Faery? Dunno. Could be an Astral buddy of my hubby, a retired Tier One Operator, or could be that I think they're cool. Help me out here. I don't know.

What about the weirdo beings who scare the holy shit out of me as I go from room to room in this house? Why is a six inch troop of faeries playing trampoline on my cat's pillow in the great room? Why did a troll slide out of the bathroom, peeking his huge head into the bedroom to see where I was? Who are the white fluffy glowing balls of ten foot whatever bouncing from one Ponderosa Pine to the next?

And I'd really appreciate an explanation of the dwarfs who shock me popping in and out of the shower. I think you get the picture. This is my life. Whenever a sweet soul says they wish they could do what I do with psychic mediumship, I wish they knew what they were really asking. No, you don't. Never say that. Sixty five years of this is a lifetime of having to adjust my inner to the outer. It started about age five or six. I'm seventy now so do the math.

That said, most of you reading this have acute psychic abilities. I know you do, so cut it out. Hiding does no good when you're talking out of both sides of your mouth, one side craving the psychic world and the other side protecting you from those who'd plop you in a dungeon for it. I know. I was in that dungeon with you. We talked about this, didn't we? So cut it out. You're safe in these writings because I know who you are. I believe in you, so you start believing more in you, my friend. These beings are there and so are you. Believe it, love it and love you.

Part of life is grieving the fact that we are here and we are, what we call, separate from divinity because we are stuck in materiality, but that's Earth school. If you look to the curriculum for Earth school, it would have all that crap in it. You would carry a backpack of the deadly sins. Have a good time.

We carry this stuff around, then we point at other people's because we see theirs, and we can't see ours on our back. But that projection, that's also part of human nature. I do that with my husband all the time. I tell him, "you're doing this, this, and this."

He says, "Zoli, you just did that."

He does it too. We all do. We go through life in this in this systemic state of terror where we're just these lost children trying to grab on to the ring. We're just going around and around and around, but that's what our school is. It is hard. You graduate from Earth school in this solar system, you get a big prize.

Earth is the only one to produce a Christ. Mars, Venus, Jupiter, Saturn, Pluto, if you want to call that a planet, and Uranus, we are the only ones to produce a Christ.

Why is that? What does that say? Because our school is so hard. When you graduate from here, you've really done something.

It takes great courage to say, "I'm going to go into Earth school, and I'm going to become an earthling for hundreds of thousands of years and endure all that." You start out like an ant. You don't know shit.

There is a group of people that were actually on Atlantis at the very beginning. We're talking ten million, fifteen million years ago on Lemuria and Atlantis. They're still here. And they want to call themselves old souls and be all hoity toity.

If that was me, I'm not telling anybody. That's embarrassing. You still don't have it right. I'm not very popular in the New Age at all because I tell people there are more like you out there. You're not a special Antlantean.

But we all go through these periods where we think we have got this all figured out. I know as soon as I think, "I got this," I watch my ego pop up, and I'll get something else thrown my way.

We all do. That's how it works. We get these breaks in between hard times, and that's when we assimilate the lessons and whatever we have. And then it's not that things get easier at all. They get harder, but we get better at handling them.

When I turn a hundred, that's thirty years away, and I'll probably make it because God will let me be here that long enough to irritate everybody. So, on my hundredth birthday, I want all the stuff that I can't have. I want a whole a bottle of Glenfiddich Scotch, I want a giant pizza with everything on it, a pack of Gitanes cigarettes, and a bag of cocaine. That's what I want when I'm a hundred because by then, I don't give a shit.

 What else do you have to do after one hundred?

We don't know, do we? We might get to leave earlier. We might get to stay longer. Depends on what kind of day we're having. You know, I've got a couple friends right now that are probably going to check out this year. Probably so. And I think, well, I'll miss them, but damn, they're free. Wow. It's interesting, isn't it?

And in the future, Maitreya says that we will celebrate at death and grieve at birth.

That's a wonderful statement. We will celebrate at death and grieve at birth. I used to have a friend who had a past life or some kind of regression where she remembered going through the birth canal. She said, "Well, here we go again."

Memento Mori

The truth is not fine-sounding; so says the *Tao Te Ching*, for everyone you know will betray you, or you will betray them.

Grieving absorbs the betrayal, the illusory feeling of abandonment, of death. Grieving is the ritual of forgetting we are mortal by allowing in the signature of death. It absolves us of forgetting that all must transition, for to remember that in constancy dilutes joy.

All things of this world have a beginning, a middle and an end. We live in between, forgetting the Memento Mori, living as though joy and pain are eternal.

To identify with the physical ends the physical. To raise awareness into the rarified air of higher frequency allows ease with transition from the middle to the end. These cycles never end. You can count on them.

Everyone you know shall die, or you will. All your possessions and accoutrements will follow that same path. Memento Mori, all things shall end except the

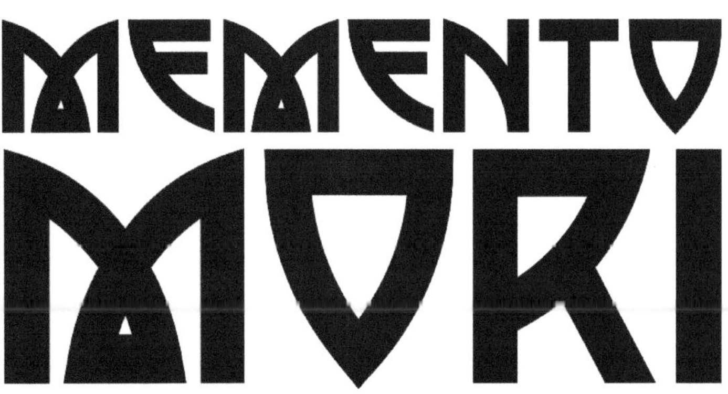

timelessness of eternity breathing through your soul.

The emotional betrayal gifted by grief is as temporary as physical life itself. Then what of it? Why try at all? Trying is the energy of manifested form. All created things of this world were thoughts before they became things. Cease to try and you cease to exist.

We are born into this world to become all things of it, then to lose it and begin again. The ensouled form spend countless lifetimes climbing the mountain only to spend a moment at the height before descending the efforted slope clothed in the realization that all that exists is Being.

What we sought is left, decaying on that other side. What we now seek is the loss of attachment to it.

The cycles of life continue until the detachment and high frequency allow the grief, the betrayal and abandonment to become absorbed by the soul's self, the tender grace breathed into the personality after centuries of lives offered in service. It comes, slowly and painfully dull at times, but detachment rests on the bottom of the sea, awaiting the awakening from the souls depths to join it in harmonious dignity with All That Is.

Life is indeed eternal, but you are not. The personality you believe is you is poisoned meat. The true you is the soul. That is eternal and knows its own consciousness. It never dies. Meditation and service is the alchemical marriage between the personality and the soul, eventually freeing the thoughts from focus upon the physical world of sensation and pain.

Happiness leads to that pain because it ends with grief when it's time is done. True joy lives in and of the soul. Memento Mori, the truth is not fine-sounding but it sets us free. Go in peace. Seek nothing and find it all.

The sacred number 7 reflects
the living tree of creativity,
born only to live and die out,
the cycle complete.

INTERDIMENSIONAL PHYSICS (IDP)

The stars were showing off tonight. Three satellites tried to compete, faking their way like plastic beauty pageant contestants verses the real deal. I lay on the deck chair overlooking my north pasture, three dogs at my feet. All was well with the world this misty October evening in Olympia. Western Washington autumn was my favorite season. The rains had returned and my Scottish Highland cattle danced gratefully in the bathing drizzle. The pastures were greening up, the gardens had harvested out.

 I lay on my chair, luxuriating in the after hours rest from fencing and pasture

maintenance that day. The only clothes I wore and even required were my dark blue sweats, hoodies, thermal shirts and several Carhart hoodie coats. No one I knew owned any rain gear, not even a rain coat. We all sported black or green rubber boots and thick socks.

Olympia mimicked Scottish moors but warmed herself by the swishing misty glow from Puget Sound's heated pools. I loved this area, my home for most of my life. The farm swam in mystic and supernatural energies, peopled with seen

and unseen beings and energies. It was my norm, whereas what I saw this evening was not too surprising, more delightful than weird.

Something was coaxing me into a dreamy density of otherworldly charm. I felt my body relax and my mind drifted. One of the dogs sighed and rolled over on her side. I found myself drifting unceremoniously in outer space. Shooting colors bounced in and out of reach as nothingness became blacker than the bottom of an ink pot. I felt myself languidly floating into a swirl of energy, something like a wind with no color but moving decidedly towards something not here. Saw a planet in the distance. It

resembled a crystal ball but had definition similar to a black rock. As I approached, I realized it was not a planet but much smaller, perhaps the size of a small house. A being was sitting on it gazing into space profound. When he turned his head, I saw he was a lovely looking man with a head larger than normal, humanoid but a bit different than that. He smiled.

In an instant, I was sitting next to him on a bench of sorts. He seemed content, perfectly at home there as though he had been sitting there for a century, which I was to learn that he had. But no time here, only space and more space.

INTERDIMENSIONAL PHYSICS (IDP)

"How do you do?" said the being, offering a well-appointed hand for me to grasp. He wore a loose fitting tunic and pants in a color I cannot describe.

"I am well," I began, grasping the offered hand. It felt surprisingly warm to the touch, surprising because I recalled no sensations since I left, where was it I'd left anyway?

"Welcome," he continued. "I am Onan. I like sitting on the edge of the universe, watching the stars go by."

Why did that sentence follow me since the 40 years ago I heard him utter it? The elegance and gravity of it has enthralled me all those years, relieved only now by having the opportunity to tell you all of this. At the time, I obediently wrote down his teaching when I awakened that next morning, still in my farm clothes and cuddled in that deck chair.

I guess you want to know what he taught me, so here we go…

WHEN IS AN OBJECT REAL IN 3 DIMENSIONS?

<u>From Onan February 16, 1980</u>

Potential Objectification

Electromagnetic wave

– thought –

All is cyclic.

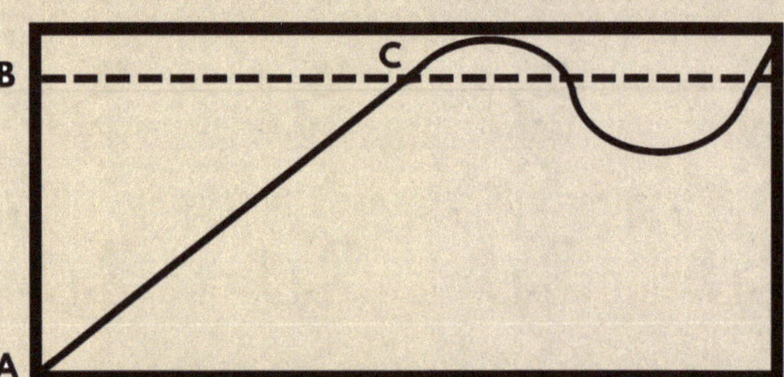

What is the exact point in time and space where (A) the abstract/electro-magnetic wave/thought energy becomes (B) a real thing in three dimensions/object-ification of thought energy/physical representation of the thing/molecules spinning in lieu of a wave?

Point A: The energy is pure in form of electro-magnetic wave

Point B: The object-ification point is reached

The point we are concerned with is so minute…it lies somewhere at point C where the pure wave energy … photons are "solidified" into an object in three dimensions:

<u>Conversation With Onan</u>

Earth Time is linear and progressive, barely functioning as a wholistic temporal measurement because of time's tendency to move forward as opposed to contra linearly. It would seem that any self-respecting *time* would move

and not

— equally...other than its Earth Time dance of two steps forward and one step back.

Emotions are frequencies. Frequencies have stable characteristics within closed systems. Closed systems may be defined as those definitive boundaries where edges overlap. Closed systems within third dimensional (and higher) realities are recognized with a surge of emotion from one identifiable feeling to another.

Free association is an example of **REALITY PIRATING** from one frequency to another, although the entity is usually resting safely within the boundaries of an agreed upon subject.

Emotions as frequencies of realities are recognized as having an entry point (−), a neutral point (±), and an exit point (+).

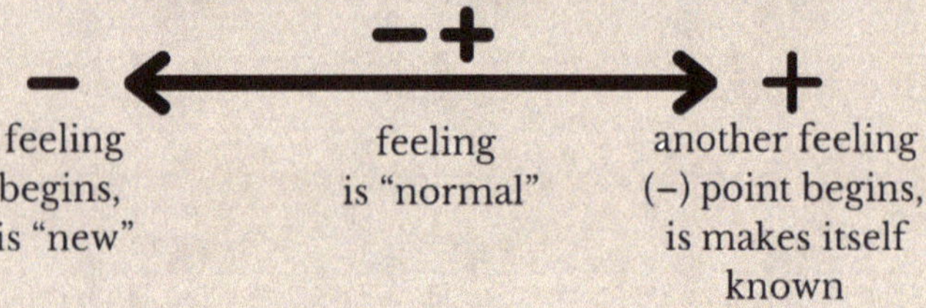

A.   At the (+) point where another feeling makes itself known, the (−) aspect of the new feeling is what magnetically draws the entity from (±) point to (+) point, and then into (−) of another feeling.

OR

B.   An inner desire pushes the energy of the feeling from (±) to (+), not magnetically as it would be drawn in A, but the (+) aspect of the (+) comes from within the entity as a "desire to experience something different."

Therefore the inner desire uses the (+) to push the feeling out into a search mode: free association of feelings drawn upon to play in the pool of available feelings until one's (−) aspect attaches onto the (+) of the previous feeling:

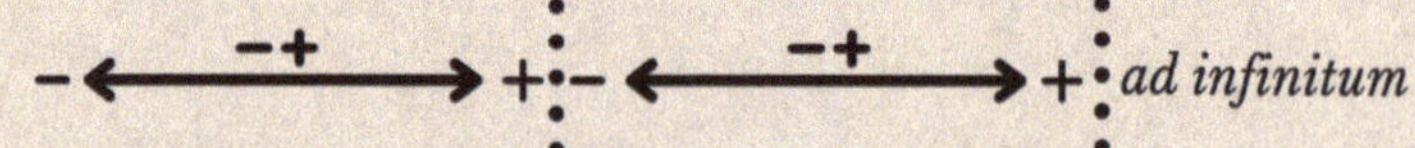

In a third dimensional reality, such shifting appears to occur linearly. In the fourth and above, it is layered, that is, it spreads outward rather than forward (futurewise) or backward (pastwise).

A		B	C
(−) (+)	to	(−) (−) (+)	(−) (+) (−)
(+) (−)	to	(+) (+)(−)	(+) (−) (+)
1 2		1 2 3	1 2 3

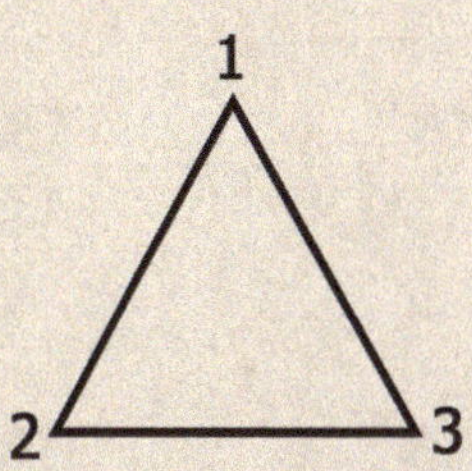

Triunity is the strongest force. One side can collapse but the other 2 are integrally connected.

Think of neg (−)/pos (+) vibrations not only as set A but as B and C potentially, for creation of M holds > potential with the 2-1, 1-2 forms of B and C as not the 1-1 of Λ. Scc?

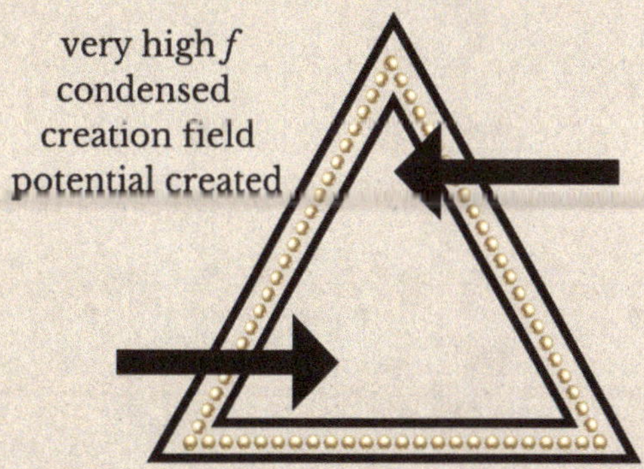

(A) Let 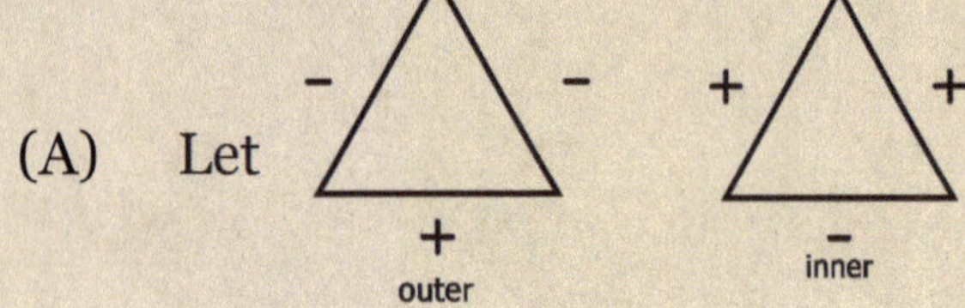 create polarity such as a

(B) current bouncing back & forth from outer to inner to, etc.

(C) Within the inner 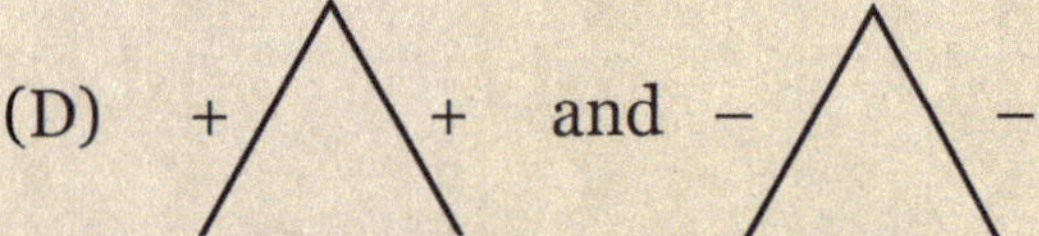 is a condensation of electrical potential, very high in f and extremely dense

(D) $+\!\!\bigwedge\!\!+$ and $-\!\!\bigwedge\!\!-$ fields at apex create a field which repels and pushes energy out apex.

(What is this?)

(E) Note also at apex where you have ( ) area you will see a peculiarity of condensation, such as (−) (+) (+) (−) field is formed which is balanced. See, the creation magnetic principle applies here because the exact point of meeting of (+) (−) (+) (−) is creation said, corporeal Mass, but said M is pushed out into reality through the apex.

In the human body,

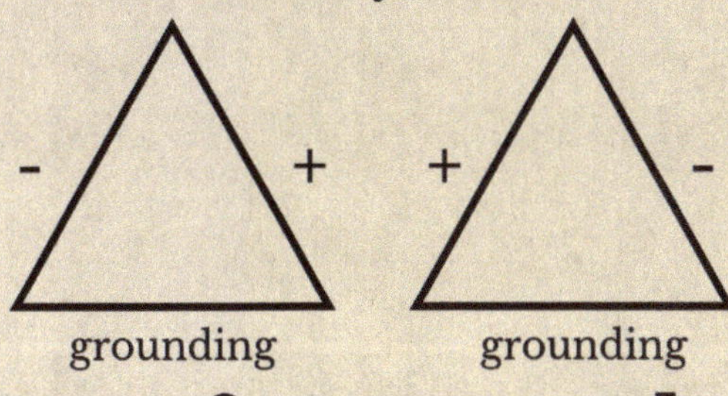

You have energy coming off the body, receptive and efferent at apex (7th seal).

Said seal being a reflective unit of conscious function is deemed the "Creator in Corpus", the Source of all creation, blessed be He/She, so deems all creation as light.

L1 current flows up to apex

L1 current flows to center bottom, grounding △

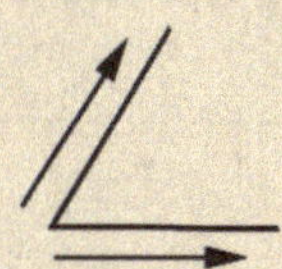

L2 current flows up to apex

L2 current flow to center bottom, grounding △

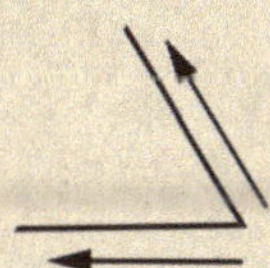

Simple.

Pyramid Base

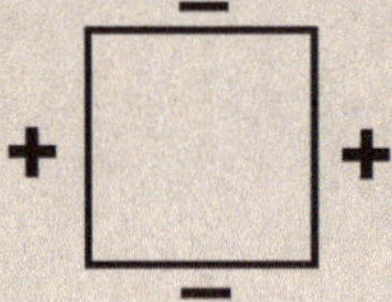

See? Current grounds 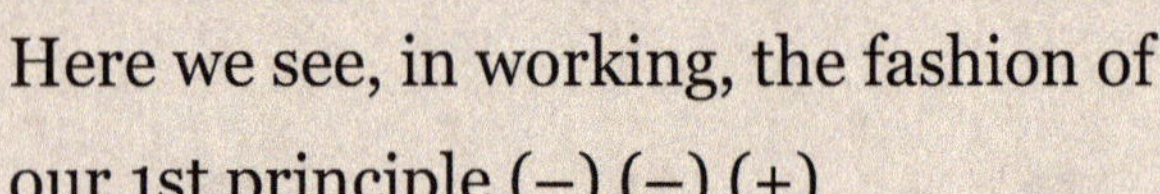

Here we see, in working, the fashion of our 1st principle (−) (−) (+)

(+) (+) (−)

the triad, triunison, <u>fortified</u> current.

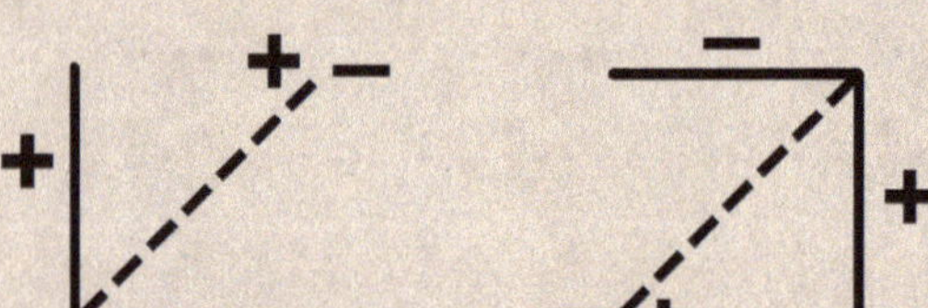 = Base

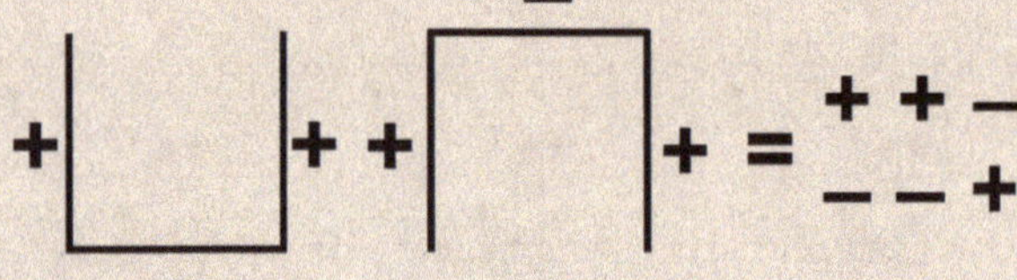 and 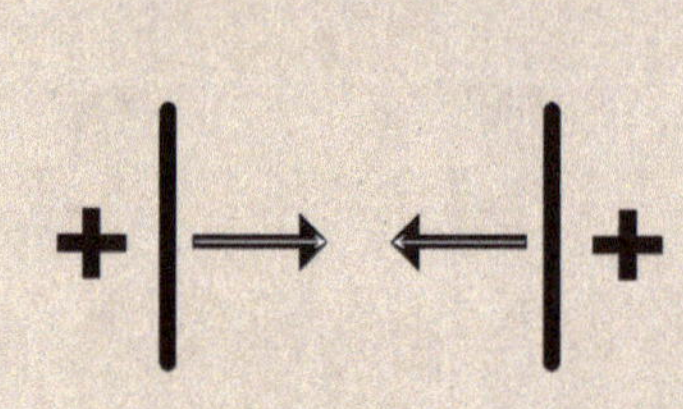 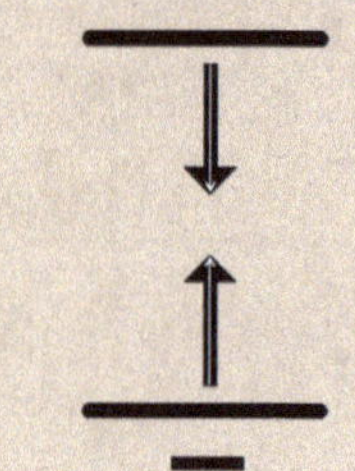

Simple

= The end result is always Love

Linda Beaulieu, you know her, she's the talent behind arranging the copy and images for Zoliart writings. We love collaboration, and I am continually humbled and delighted by her gifts unfolding and presenting my words to you.

So much of my work is not for me, but for you, whomever you are. I just get-er-out there. Linda experienced a breakthrough in her dream time which amazed and delighted my doubting self. Why do I doubt? I feel like a fish flopping around powerlessly on a lonely beach when I dream. No skill to change anything, I just don't possess that talent. But Linda accessed intel from Onan to change her reality. I cajoled her into including it here. I'm not beyond whining like a two year old to get my buddies to agree, lol! See what you think!

After working on the Onan IDP article, my night was filled with dreams. And as the info and formulas replayed in my mind, I realized I could change my dreams while they happened. In one dream, I lost my computer and was looking through a complex of buildings, anxious to find it.

Then, I remembered I could change the frequency of my reality so that my computer was right where I wanted. It became clear that whatever part of the dream I didn't like, I felt a "desire to experience something different." And in that intense moment or feeling, I was able to pull in a different reality. The energy of the emotion was what propelled it.

While arranging this information, I came across an image of a Merkabah aligned with a body (on page 78). Well, that led me to look deeper into the origin and meaning of Merkabah as it is something I am familiar with, but not an expert on. What I found was that the Merkabah works the way Onan described. It would be incredible to hear your thoughts.

Q: I'm trying but don't believe any of this unconscious or Faery stuff. Where do you get this? I just don't believe in it.

A: You are right. I agree with you. You don't believe it. This is not your field of interest or education and perhaps your work is to monitor things accessing only the five physical senses. We need you doing that. I understand and pray you continue your zetetic approach to the paranormal. We need you doing that.

Here's an example, this should help. My Tier One Operator, Spec Opps hubby is similar to your energy field. He'll tolerate my rambling and politely listen to my psychic stuff before saying, "Is there any more of that chicken?" He works in Earth areas as a retired military operator and currently on a SWAT team. He's a master in those areas and loves me enough to stand in the doorway of the room I'm psyching in, but maintain his own boundaries.

Belief IN these supernatural things is not a requisite to living a full life. Do you know who Winston Churchill was, the erudite British statesman of the last century? Winnie was a fourth degree initiate and had zero interest in the supernatural. He thought it was rubbish. Did his disinterest mean it actually was rubbish? Nope. That was his belief, but his belief did not define the experience of others.

We stay in our lane and do what is in front of us if we want to succeed in life. Not that hard, until distractions and sensory temptations throw the emotional switch. Whatever you are passionate about, be it electronics, science, religion, service...whatever that is, go there. Well, go there if it is allowing light into your life.

What does it mean to you to be alive? We come into form to learn about form. Once we know how to control form, we grow out of this school into a pure light body devoid of astral problems.

Here's an idea...did I create the Reality Pirate or was it already there, and I tripped over it to find it? What you doubt about all this stuff is the frequency signature that will lead you into the room with the answers you seek. Trust that. It's real.

Q: I'm confused about the 5th Dimension and how we're supposed to be there. How do I get there?

A: Everything's there forever. Remember how everything is energy? All is happening right now, past , present, and future are a cohesive whole. That's all there is. We nit pick ourselves into the tight corner of a Saturnian labeling drama by agreeing to limit consciousness with what we call time.

The New Age religion is based on fanciful imagination. There is much beauty and some truth there but you are guilted into lacking god-like abilities, shamed when you are sick, denied access to logic and thrown about like a rag doll with the constantly changing winds billowing the sails of the New Age vessel. You are enough, you know.

There is no way to "get to" the 5th dimension here because time does not exist. Indeed you can access different frequencies and various densities, but these are personal experiences. Can you share those with others? The frequencies, yes, densities, no. Time is a teacher of Saturn and karma. Time is a limiting boundary giving experiential form to your emotional rollercoaster called life. You've done this all before, a lot in fact, so here you go again.

Maybe this will help; the first Dimension is symbolized by a dot. The dot joins other dots and becomes a straight line. That's the symbol for the second dimension.

What comes next? The third is a cube, which is a physically recognized form. Moving, that's the fourth. The fifth is more conscious awareness of those four, see? Is there a sixth? Yes, but fuhgeddaboudit. You can't access that either.

In my experience, those sweet folks trying to convince me that they are in the 5th Dimension are the same ones whose bank account is overdrawn and they were stuck at home for two weeks with a rhinovirus and high fever. But now they're in the mystical world in which you, normal person, can neither reach nor breathe their rarified air. Nope, you're just too humble and normal living out a good life in the old non spiritual 3D.

But wait! They'll help you become them once you do what they say is the flavor of the month spiritual practice. Surely, you know what that is. The latest is judgement. In the 5th dimensional New Age religion you can no longer judge or you are bad. Bad normal person! If you broach the subject and question, God forbid, use your skill of discernment called judging, you will be gossiped about and looked down upon by the 5th Dimensional Devotees.

QUIS UT DEUS, Michael challenged Satan as he was thrown to the abyss. So goes the story. Mater Divina, the Divine Mother of eternal receptive intuition now breathes life into old forms.

Hate has an end date to it. Love doesn't. You can't have too much love. It's what holds everything together. I was thinking about that today, and it's not the emotion of, "oh, I feel love."

There's something deeper and much quieter and eternal, and that's what love is. It's the glue that holds everything together, everything.

And we have to destroy the old forms for the new to come in. It is frightening, and it's debilitating, and forms die. That's what the Masters refer to as desecration of forms, getting rid of forms, making way for the new ones to come in. Sometimes, you have to kill the body to save the soul. And not everything is karmic, but it can become that.

In other words, if somebody is born in an in a very difficult part of the world like Haiti, it can be said that they had the

misfortune of being born in just an unfortunate place.

It's not always karmic, but it can be karmic and it can become that in the sense that you can evolve and grow from that and create some good. And suffering of others reflects on the suffering of the self. It's always the self that is suffering. It's the part that's changing.

Ray One is suffering, destruction, and it is destroying of comfort or anything that is solid that we think it is going to be forever because it's not.

The only thing that's forever is the soul and God, and we already know all of that. Anything that you can visibly see or anything connected with the five physical senses, that's going away. That's a tool for this lifetime, and it's a tool for other people, and it's how we evolve and grow and spiritualize matter.

Some people don't seem to grow in this lifetime as much as others and there are so many reasons for that. Maybe they're just not interested in living in a locale unsupportive of such growth. Perhaps they aren't surrounded by or grow up with people that encourage that, or any reason you can think of. But, usually, when the soul becomes more important than the personality, when we've lived thousands and thousands and thousands of lives, we start to see there is more than this physical world.

What is it? We start to search, and we start to seek, something other than, and that's when the search begins. And then there are thousands of lives and we begin to see the older souls are the ones that are bringing the other ones up behind them, so to speak. I didn't say that right, but I think you know what I mean. There's consciousness to that.

The young souls seem like it's taking them longer, but it's really they just haven't awakened to it yet. There's still the physical and it takes all of us more than one lifetime to get there.

And there are people on this planet that aren't really old souls, but they've had thousands, if not millions, of lives in other star systems. But when you come here, you have to start over with Earth rules. It's like all of a sudden, I'm going to school in Iraq. Really? Do you speak Farsi? Do you know the customs? Do you know can you eat something called food? It's a brand new you in a new situation.

And Earth's school is the hardest one in the solar system. You really do evolve and

grow from this. And as I've said before, Earth is the only planet in our solar system to produce a Christ.

For some people, the environment is so different that they feel alien. Even though a DNA test would validate their humanness, they call themselves aliens. I know how that feels

There are so many explanations for that. I think mainly when we see that, it's just people that don't fit well into society they're born into for whatever reason.

What is a young soul? What is an old soul? I can't really answer that, but we think that wiser people are older souls. We tend to think that whether it's true or not. And then there are the avatars. An

avatar is a being who fell to Earth, to serve.

That'd be Michelangelo. That'd be Moses, Abraham Lincoln. These are rare beings. Many of them are from Venus. They're very highly evolved. But guess what? They come to Earth and they have to start at the beginning here. And by the time they reach the point of being able to serve like Michelangelo, they have lived thousands of lives here.

I joke and say most of us are just dumb. We come back over and over again because we take a while to get stuff done.

Maybe I really wanted to learn to play golf. Great. Next time, I'll be born in Scotland and have a really shitty life for forty years before I get hit in the head with a golf ball and die. We do stuff like that. We really do. It's just ridiculous. The truth is much stranger than anything we can make up.

I really believe that anything you can imagine, anything is out there. Anything. The imagination is very powerful. We create image and action, abstract ideals to where we can think, you know, I bet I have been a horse before. No, you have never been a horse, I guarantee you. And you will never be a horse. That's called transmigration of souls. You humans do not become animals. Animals do not become humans. However, in between lifetimes, maybe you ventured into the consciousness of a horse for a little bit.

It could be a dolphin. It could be anything like that, but you will not be born into anything but a human.

My father used to say he wanted to come back as one of my animals. You know? And, comically, my nephew's fiancée named their dog Marvin, daddy's name. So, maybe he came back as a dachshund. I don't know.

Reality is very plastic. It's very movable, and we count on, as I've written before, we count on things being solid. The chair, I hope to God it's going be a chair when I go sit in it, and it's not morphed into a swimming pool. There are certain things that are constructs, that are solid, that are agreed upon, and I don't think we should spend a lot of time trying to pretend they're not.

But the imagination can go anywhere and do anything. We come from this reality of things not being physical. And kids until

they're about nine that are usually psychically open. Don't parents sometimes wonder, where the heck they got some of the things they intuit?

It's amazing. And then they lose it, and then they become of the world. It's all hormones and it's all the age that you're at, and you do have to evolve and grow into that.

It's the comedy of Thom and I watching our friends with their kids that now they're thirty, they have a kid, and they

have to adult. That's the verb. You have to adult, which takes place in the physical world.

On one hand, you don't need money, money is considered evil, but only because it is so physically enticing. Fine. But you have to pay rent. You need insurance. You have to buy food. As with everything, there is a balance to it. You can approach it with love instead of labelling it.

Newsflash! Attention all Martian and Pleiadian concubines assigned to Earth presidents and world leaders. It has come to our attention that you are not taking precautions to protect yourself.

We are tired of warning you, so this will be your final reprieve. Do not, we repeat, do not add beans to Earth chili!

The concoction known as a south western delicacy has proven the downfall of countless concubines over the last several centuries. Once ingested with earth beans added, you will become formidable in *foul scent*, forcing yourself to retreat to the room of relief missing pertinent opportunities from said careless action on your part, in the presence of those you are assigned to control.

We can not repeat this enough. Leave the beans to the *world leaders* who are already full of what that substance produces.

Do you understand that the unseen is eternal and that supernatural Beings are uncountable? It is not yet understood that the invisibly exquisite unseen bathes everyday life in a sublime aura of experience. You are surrounded daily, each night, with billions of Beings from the size of an atom to greater than our sun. Does this surprise you? Do you wonder why you cannot see them with your physical eyes?

Icky Beings are part of the reality of unseen thingies making life uncomfortable. But here's the deal…like attracts like. The more you clear past stuff from your life, the greater you raise and cleanse your body, mind and spirit, the less attractive you'll be to the icky beings. True dat. What makes some folks so delicious to bad luck and repetitively awful experiences? Is it their fault? Probably not, but here's the deal. Who are your friends? Where do you go in the public arena? What stimulation do you crave? Hanging out in bars, casinos, low level music areas...that is where the Icky Ones go. You're in the presence of the awful and wonder why you feel awful.

This is obvious but is apparently ignored and not known. You can't apply physical rules and laws to non physical beings and phenomena. The rules are different. You can't measure supernatural energy with material instruments tuned to measure the physical world. We go through periods of deception and believe that the bizarre is truth and the simple is a lie. Dogs do not want to become cats nor can they.

Christina Morrison

The following pages contain depictions of beings created through collaboration as Zoli described her experiences and Christina illustrated them.

Christina Morrison is an artist and illustrator who delights in drawing the subject matter portrayed in these images. Drawn to healing through art and other means, she recently received her certification in Hypnotherapy and Past Life Regression to continue facilitating beauty and health through all possible means. She resides in Northern California with her husband and three children.

94

The Clipboard People

1978 in Nashville, Tennessee found me locked into a tight Spirit-imposed daily schedule of being schooled by Those Who Guard and Guide me. That's my own label for the Theosophical and non-physical teachers guiding my schooling and education in my field of metaphysics and mystic arts.

I distinctly recall awakening one summer day to see two males standing at the foot of my bed. They looked to be around thirty years of age, light colored, short hair and fair skin, sporting white over-shirts and cream colored pants. They were both holding traditional clip boards with white paper. They each had a pen or pencil, undefined, and looked at me in a detached manner.

The one to my left said "This is Zoli and she gets up at 07:30." I then fully awakened out of my astrally focused state and wondered why I was clearly observed like a patient in a hospital. As I continued on with my day, I did not feel them accompany the teachers and Beings apparently assigned to deal with my schooling at that time. Please note that

I've addressed this difficult period in my life in several other of my books.

Over the years, I have seen a single Clipboard Person in my times of need. For example, at my farm in Olympia I sometimes asked for help in organizing appointments for my small fold of Scottish Highland cattle. Since leaving the farm, I see a single Clipboard Person when Spirit wants my attention in certain areas of my life. There's no definitive timing or situation which calls them in, as I no longer request their help. But who or what are they? I am told they are "part of

Hierarchy, Beings who arrange, organize and act as go-betweens for people and their Guidance." They always look the same to me whereas I intuit they could be projected thought forms, non-physical and wholly Astral who appearance, non-threatening to those who see them. If so, they are under the direction of higher Beings desiring specific things to be accomplished in the physical, which is our life on Earth.

Artist: Christina Morrison

The Angry Boy

Several years ago I was puttering around downstairs and happened to glanced out the glass doors leading into the back yard. I was taken aback to see what appeared to be an angry little boy. This upset guy had short dark hair, medium toned skin and was dressed in dark colored shorts and a light colored loose shirt.

He looked to be no older than maybe ten. His eyes, though dark, were not black like the fabled Black Eyed Children. I wondered if he was lost because although angry, he looked sad. He stared at me through the glass and wanted me to know how upset he was. Clearly angry.

His appearance scared me because I very rarely see angry or Beings from the Involutionary Arc of Devas, as they are negative and belong to the solid structure arc of holding matter in place. That is what we define as evil. Devas can be from the Evolutionary or the Involutionary Arc.

I found myself disconcerted and said out loud "Nope, no way you're coming inside this house."

I felt myself back up a bit and then observed two female looking faeries approach him, pleading with him to do something. He hung his head and clenched his fists, reluctantly listening to their pleads to go somewhere with them.

All three of these Beings were about four feet tall with the second female a bit shorter. She hung back a bit while the taller Faery spoke with angry boy in a calm manner. The Faeries were garbed differently. The one who spoke with him wore a little colorful skirt with triangle edges, bells on the points and

Artist: Christina Morrison

glimmering top. She held nothing in her hands and wore no hat.

I wonder now if she knew him because they resembled each other. Was he part of her troupe? The smaller Faery wore a long white dress, had wavy blonde long hair and a glimmer fog emanating from the top of her head. Maybe she was there for emotional support...an emotional support Faery!

I was relieved to see Angry Boy walk off with them, disappearing in a misty waft of wind from the right side of the house. Who was he? I have no idea but felt he was up to no good. Have you seen anyone like this?

Artist: Christina Morrison

Guardian Trolls – Gwop

I first recall becoming aware of these guys after we moved to the Montana woods in 2013. As with many remote mountain homes in Montana, our house was crafted on a clearing nestled in between several mountains surrounding a gulch. In the Deep South we called them hollers, but here they are gulches. In the flatlands, the Rocky Mountain areas are filled with topsoil washed from the mountains over centuries of weather changes.

The Missoula area was actually a huge glacial lake. Our mountain residence would have been waterfront property. This prehistoric proglacial lake was formed during the last ice age about 13,000 to 15,000 years ago. It was about 3,000 square miles in size and held half the volume of fresh water of present Lake Michigan. I bet the fishing was great!

But I digress. Our on-the-side-of-a-mountain residence lacked yard and planting areas save a small grassy front yard and similarly small back area. We hired Carras Nursery in town to construct "the Great Wall of Missoula," offering

now lovely terraced areas for planting and lovely space for wildlife.

Underneath our deck there is a portal I became aware of after peering over the deck and seeing a wavering energy similar to water rippling. I ventured down to the area, scrambled over the rocky scree and felt a tingle down my left side. What is this? A gnome wavered. I saw nothing psychically or visually so I filed it away for further research.

Several evenings later I was awakened by a peculiar smell and rather large energy field emanating from the portal in our dressing area ten feet from my side of the bed. The smells associated with Beings are usually dissimilar from those I identify with my nose. These smells, although located a bit below my forehead and directly in between my eyebrows, can remind me of known smells but only that. They are non physical and emanate from non physical Beings.

There he was. A seven foot, chunky bodied troll dude holding a shovel. I squeezed my eyes a bit to make out his

figure in the scant moonlight sneaking through the glass doors.

"Can I dig a tunnel in the wall?" I psychically heard him say.

"You what?" I sat up in bed, clearly awake, staring at the weird smelling troll staring at me rather gently, for a troll, that is. More on them later.

"Why do you want to dig a tunnel? Where exactly?" seemed the right thing for me to ask.

The troll shifted and moved the shovel into his other hand. As he did, I smelled even more of the, well, troll aroma.

"You built a wall right in the traditional transfer area." he began. "We need it

reopened so things can get from here to there." Was he upset? I didn't want an angry troll in our bedroom at 1:00 a.m.

"Oh wow. I see. You're right. I didn't check I with any or you Beings before we did that. Now I'm embarrassed and feel awful."

The troll stared at me as though nothing I said made any sense since Troll is not my native tongue.

"I'll go dig now." He turned away and disappeared.

That was weird, I got out of bed and wandered through the dark rooms, finally reaching the other deck area near the verboten wall. I saw him digging at a furious pace through the huge manor blocks and into the terraced area of the hill. Hmmm. Who is this guy, I mused.

"I'm Gwop." I heard psychically. I began picking up intel on his kind, that they are not the traditional under-the-bridge irascible dumb trolls, but evolved later to be workers for other Beings. They're actually very sweet and perhaps more aware than other of the worker Beings out there. They like to help, are earthy and crazy strong, and eat a mineral in rocks

Artist: Christina Morrison

and feed on some element from the sun I cannot name.

I padded back into the bedroom and drifted off to a dreamless sleep devoid of trolls or walls. After my morning coffee I chanced examining the tunnel area he'd created. True to Gwop's word, I psychically saw multiple Beings of varied natures wandering in and coming out of his opening which looked to be no more than four feet in diameter. He'd set native rock around the perimeter as a lovely castle wall would appear in maybe a study book. This guy had skills!

Okay, I hear you. What other Beings use the tunnel? Ten years after its creation I still see trolls, golden light Beings of the Faery kingdom, tiny horses, faeries and the traditional gnomes and dwarfs, but not all at the same time. I try to leave the area alone psychically in an offering of respect for their work. But is it a coincidence that I experience supernatural events in the garden area directly above the tunnel path? Dunno. What do you think?

Artist: Christina Morrison

<u>Fuzzy Dude</u>

June 29, 2024 at 10:38 pm. As I lay in bed I psychically saw a three foot Being approach me as I lay on the left side of our bed near my multiple altars area. This is where I do sleep. The small smiling Being was covered in gentle brown fur not unlike a furry dog. I clearly heard him joyfully exclaim "We're furry!" Delighted, I smiled at him and said intuitively "Yes, you really are fuzzy. Glad to meet you. I see only one of you."

"I'm the bravest of all." he replied, standing with his left hand touching the quilt. He had human looking hands and fingernails which looked to be brown like the fur covering his hands and fingers. He was indeed fuzzy from head to foot. I say foot because he had precious tiny cloven hooves like you'd think Pan might have.

I put down my iPad and looked at his delightedly friendly demeanor, curious who he was. "I've never seen your kind before," thinking he was definitely not one of the dwarfs or gnomes, both who look different from each other and unfurry at that.

"What are you called?" I requested while hearing birdsong from outside the open

Artist: Christina Morrison

window while hearing him say "Something like that. Our name is not translatable."

I recall pondering how to identify him with some definable word when he said "Just think of that birdsong, that is who we are."

I then drifted off to sleep and dreamed of seeing The Magician character from my book holding a long leash with a dog on the end. I didn't see what kind of dog it was but it was black. They were standing alone on a huge paved area similar to an empty lot. I saw them from a Bird's Eye view, from above.

When I awakened this morning I pondered the last night's events and recalled at dusk seeing and hearing a bird slam into the huge plate glass window. "Oh no!" I said, rushing downstairs to see a swallow lying wings spread out on the concrete. As I always do, I gently lifted him and felt he was breathing slightly. I prayed over him, invoking Christ and saying Maitreya's name 7 times which is an exorcism. I continued cradling him, praying over him and projecting the green healing light into the thin violet auric field around him. I visualized him flying healthfully off. I guess I did this for about 10 minutes when I felt him move slightly. A minute later, I removed one hand and saw him fly off.

This morning I connected the furry fellow and the bird song name and the Bird's Eye view of the Magician. The Magician tarot card is my "card for this life" which I connect with Ray 7. Yesterday was a Saturday, Aratron's day. He gives familiars and is my teacher in the Olympic Spirits. Hmmm. It usually takes time for these things to create conscious paths forward for me. But the furry guy was certainly not silent like the dwarfs and the gnomes who only project visuals and words into my mind. This guy was vibrant. With his Devic tiny hooves and fur I presume he is connected with the Bird Tribes. I'll let this first article go and tell you more later.

It answers nothing these days to comment that things are weird. We are weird, things are as they are. As I sat commiserating over these events and what I could possibly do to direct the new Beings and be of assistance to them, I felt a warmth come over me which connected me with the Other, my word for other people, other Beings, other unknown entities. I realized on a deeper level that not only are we never alone but perhaps crave aloneness due to the constant and ever presence of Those Who Guard And Guide Us. Is it truly that or do we simply forget that?

Later on today, Sunday, I spoke with my Body/ Emotion/ Belief Code practitioner. As we located and cleared several stuck

emotions I psychically heard one of my smart-ass Guidance say "That's just the cost of doing business these days." Gee, don't hold back.

His point was a stab at my rooting around in emotions even after they are cleared. I do that. Are the furry Beings here to serve a spot of joy? It feels like that. This little guy was enlivening, joy filled and seeking connection. Sometimes we cannot understand things so we just explain what we do. That's not feeling. This fur fellow was bursting with feeling. I'm curious where it is going, yet suspect he is part of The Joy Bringer (Maitreya's) group. We shall see.

Moon Faced Beings

Is he sad or just sweetly curious? I glanced over towards the portal in our dressing room area to see a very round faced adorable cutie. He was no more than two feet tall with latte colored skin and the roundest, fattest face I'd ever seen. He peered at me and made a boo boo face as though I'd hurt his feelings. I continued to stare at this guy and realized his boo boo face was his resting fat face. Delightful but rather disconcerting.

"What am I now to do with you?" I began. I saw his eyes squint as though to squeeze out a tear, but realized yet again, this was his normal him. I looked down at my iPad for a second perhaps to see if he'd still be there when I looked back. Gone. No fat face kiddo.

Last night I was in our gym downstairs, trying to concentrate on the treadmill drama for at least another 30 minutes. Our cat, Sophia Montana, padded downstairs to scratch and stretch on the gym carpet. A couple Bronze tom turkeys wandered past the double glass doors behind the treadmill, craning their

elegant necks to peer through the glass. Mercifully the late afternoon sun was on the opposite side of the house preventing the interlopers from seeing their reflection in the glass and commence pecking at the supposed enemy. Several times a week either Thom or I venture downstairs to wave our arms at the glass preventing them from potentially breaking their beaks.

Sophia relinquished her post at the weight bench and curled up to comfy it out until I was done. Not again. Who was that? The wall mirror reflected the dumbbell rack and I psychically saw a Being borrowing the material structure of the bench to manifest. Have you seen this

happen? Here's how it works: A non physical Being wants to appear physical and borrows physical objects or even things in nature to give them form. It's all matter, after all. They drop frequency from the etheric level. There are 4 levels above solid, liquid and physical gas. We talked about this, you recall, and we'll address it at length later on but I know you get it because you've seen things out of the corner of your eye that appear real but then look like just a chair or a tree, right?

But I digress. A chubby moon faced female stood beseeching me to communicate. But how? Just like her

Artist: Christina Morrison

male counterpart she seemed sad, hurt, curious, maybe just dumb. Is that what's going on? I have never seen anyone like them and they seem non physical. Nuts. I don't get it.

I focused on my exercise and watched Sophia Montana grab a toy before trotting happily into Thom's shop. I love to watch Netflix series during exercise periods and forgot about the little Beings. I guess detaching sometimes clears my mind. The full moon started peeking over the mountain, offering a little mystery to the realistic cop show on Netflix.

Ah ha! I got it! These moon faced Beings are low level manifestations of tonight's full moon in Cancer. They apparently borrowed thought forms from the available etheric library to manifest. Dunno. I'm always surprised to see Beings and even more surprised by what they do in our physical, which is their unnatural world. Even flower faeries work with the etheric psychic forms of the flowers which are identical to the ones we see. Are these Moon Beings etheric lunar projections? What do you think?!

Psychopomp

One of, if not THE most disturbing Being I have encountered reminds me of the Dementors out of Harry Potter. JK Rowling was apparently in touch with some deep stuff to create that magnificent series, teaching kids that not all is good and most things have a dark side. That said, she empowered them with the promise of what we in Theosophy recognize as Ray 7, Ceremonial Order and Ritual Magic. The Age of Aquarius, now, will embody more of these energies as more soul Ray 7 folks come into bodies. But I digress.

If it was a dream it was a dark one. If it was an otherworldly sort of Out of Body Experience (OOBE), that would make more sense. I still don't know for sure, but I recall one rainy winter afternoon with darkness rolling in around 3:30 as it did

in Western Washington. At my Farm I'd often nap after feeding in the afternoon. This was one of those days.

The only way to make any sense of this is to tell you that I felt drugged, but I did not drink or do any drugs. Wasn't my deal. I recall lying down and feeling woozy, dizzy but in a way that felt like rolling in and out of my physical body. I recall feeling like I was surrounded with a pressure that smelled blacker than black. As weird as it sounds, all my senses seemed to be running together. I couldn't move but felt unafraid, irrationally so since I intuited I

was now in the first Astral level we call hell. It was as though time was frozen and I saw me looking at me in a third or fourth person way. I became aware of a depressingly foreboding energy field grabbing at my gut, the third chakra of emotion. I then both felt, saw and heard a voice happening at the same time. But it seemed to be saying words backwards as I saw a dark field appear in a mirror. The reversal of field energy straightened out but turned everything upside down. I felt nauseous. The voice and sight straightened out and this is what it said….

"Tempted by my lower nature I fell apart at the seams, tearing sinew from bone, my aura dissipated in the winds of time. Naught but loss enveloped my soul, bereft of succor, absent of joy, the drawing down of lunar darkness soaked dry the intended potion, leaving me hanging by a thread cast off from the garment left behind. No one heard me, no one sought me, not even my own soul.

"Darkness ensued and billowed the sails of discontent voyaging upon dank seas ripe with the sins of mankind. My lower nature knew me better than my soul, and caressed the emptiness within with promises of a death-relieving act of contrition. Naught behind it, nothing ahead, the creaking silence of the eternal present promised nothing. Nothing at all.

"I leave you now with a warning: That those who hate you seek not your demise but your light. Those who bother you request your divine intervention. My lower nature forgot this even as it was pressed upon my blackening heart. No one came to save me, for saving was the grace denied those refusing to save themselves with forgiveness.

"I reach out to you now from the bowels of this forlorn place, still unforgiving of myself and locked in a place with no key. Heed well these words, for I will never utter them again. I am not allowed. Seek continually the tiniest glimmer of light and hope, for even that shall gain strength

with your attention upon it. I leave you now."

How did recall this? I wrote it down immediately after exiting the awful place. I recall feeling voraciously hungry and parched. Clearly I was taken to "hell" to be given a message. It felt like a ghost from Ebenezer Scrooge in *A Christmas Carol*. I looked at the bedside clock to see only two minutes had passed, in this reality at least. I felt like the experience was hours long. Awful. Just awful.

I never clearly saw the poor soul who had damned himself to "hell" out of guilt and the choice to not forgive his human frailties. He just seemed like a tar pit figure, does that make sense? That was by far the most disconcerting Being I've met.

The Collectors...Black Blob

Have you ever waited in traffic from a wreck up ahead? What happens to all the understandably negative emotions and painful feelings hanging back during and after the event? I considered just that yesterday while watching flashing lights and first responders several blocks ahead of me. Nobody needs that, is what I always say to myself, sending light and blessings to all involved.

Artist: Christina Morrison

But where do all those emotions go? Energy created indeed never disappears, so where does it go? I passed by the scene and went on my way, only to return an hour later to see the cleared scene appearing as though nothing had happened. But what was that?! A swirling and blurring of air revealed a funnel and sweeping motions around the wreck area. It reminded me of fast forwarding a movie. The Beings were undefinable, formless yet somehow popping in and out of form, both ghostly and ethereal. As I wondered who and what they were I heard the word "Collectors". Have you ever had a download phase in so quickly that you knew the message of paragraphs-long info all at once? That's what happened. I learned that these Beings had no form proper but borrowed thought images from observers as though to lend understanding about their existence. I felt no emotion or human connection, simply felt they were doing what they were created to do.

The download revealed these beings as part of Ray 1, the destroyer aspect who end and clean up used and unneeded energies allowing the new to birth. Does

that make sense? There are countless numbers of these Collectors. They are magnetically drawn to battle fields, death sites, but more interestingly anywhere negative emotions are released en mass. They cart off or dissipate these energies.

I've never considered either the existence or necessity of such things, but now wonder what life on earth would be like without them. How many wars, wrecks, icky emotions get stuck in energy fields, poisoning locations, until these Collectors remove them? The world would otherwise be a thick goo of negativity,

Artist: Christina Morrison

blocking the healing and illuminating frequency of fresh forms unless this was cleared. Again, these Beings had neither form nor consciousness save the purposeful intent and energy field of their Being.

(part 2)

The last few days found me emerged in Plutonian death and dead energies. Can't explain it, but I found it more interesting than irritating. Our cat, Sophia Montana devised to hunt and kill two birds, three chipmunks and two of my favorite squirrels. Not that I can tell the remaining

body parts from each other, but it caused pause as I refrained from scolding her catly self. I psychically heard a voice reporting that there were '"too many squirrels in this area" so they allowed it. Go figure. I closed the tiny terror in the house for a day and cleaned up some arterial spray of blood on the carpet in our dressing room where she likes to hang over her kill like Gollum and his precious.

That evening as I passed close to the area I psychically saw a long, shiny black human-shaped thing laying still on the kill zone. It looked slug like with vaguely definable features, like a four-foot piece of melting licorice. Weird. I asked "May I walk through you?"

"I'd prefer you didn't." The blob responded. As I tuned into the field, I saw it was a thought form collection of ideas and beliefs from my mind, representing the death Ray 1 aspect. What's with all this death stuff right now? As with everything else, this too shall pass. Even Pluto needs a break some time. The next morning found neither carcass nor slimy black blob on the carpet. Welcome to my life.

Q: Are Creatures like Centaurs and the Sphinx mythological? Are they imaginary? Are they some mad scientist's daydream?

A: Well, I think there can be different answers for different things. The centaur is a being created in Atlantean times from people and animals.

The demonic forces of Materiality, of evil, started mixing humans and animals. And these were miserable, miserable creatures. They were finally sent to a healing center called The Temple Beautiful to be given solace and emotional help.

And I don't know if they could be turned into one or the other. I'm not sure. But it was truly a miserable existence as a being who didn't know what they were and they were half in between, and the consciousness was not right.

But they were absolutely real and existed as evilly created to serve the pleasures of the few conscious humans controlling everyone else. Not a lot of evolved people lived then. But those created creatures were not evil themselves.

And there were some that were very wise, Chiron, who was the healer, the doctor healer. He healed many people, but he couldn't heal himself. And so in astrology, Chiron, the centaur, wherever your Chiron placement is in your chart, that is where you can help others, but you can't help yourself.

The sphinx was created at the time when the Atlanteans escaped to Egypt before the destruction of that continent because it had gone so astray from The Plan. That is Ray One, as you recall. It's because the old has to be destroyed for the new to come in.

In other words, the things from Atlantis came and created Egypt. So, the Sphinx came from Atlantean ideas into Egypt, and it stands for the man and the lion, which is the constellation Leo in the sky. There's a lot written on that, and I'm not sure the entirety of it. We do see in Hindu mythology, the representation of these human-animal god ideas.

A lot of that just stands for the consciousness of those two things coming together.

The sacred 7 again, supported by the trinity of divine promise that all is Love. Who are you and where do you rest your creativity when not in use?

The material world is a neutral palate and we add emotion to it. The neutrality of materiality expresses as all things being the same until we add reactive response to the physical.

Detachment presents the clarity of watching the show while participating only when necessary. The limbic system and the astral body are the culprits of reactivity, adding fear, apprehension, projection and all the emotions of control as we seek comfort from the resolution of opposites.

But what's a girl to do? We're in a body to BE in a body, to express and react, respond and intuit to the delight of the soul who is a Master on its own plane. Our personality, emotional and mental bodies are the playing field while the emotions are the ball in play.

Do Supernatural Beings feel? Do they play on that same field or do they press onto it their own designs, disrupting the equanimity of human efforting? What do you think?

Many years ago I met on the astral planes, a delightful Yoda-like character who called himself Chin Lao. He appeared

always as a smiling Chinese aged man, sitting comfortably, garbed in robes of the ancient periods. He told me stories, aphorisms, and challenged me to quit fence-sitting, to learn and discern my own value system. He spoke often of the delightful illusion of congealed matter, when energy dropped frequency and collected molecules from the ethers to become visible to the physical sense of sight.

The tactile nature of things presented as I learned the proper placement of objects in my home and garden. I have since learned that is called the Feng Shui path.

He taught me that things get moved around until they find where they live. That's why it's wise to gift away all things that no longer live with you. All things have their time and their placement. There is an art to sensitizing yourself to this field. It is super sensory and not found with the five physical senses. Use your spider senses. They are real!

The energy signature of channeled reception is quite different from those of the fourth chakra or above. I can't really explain it except it's very emotional. The differences are acute. I'm not a fan of anyone following channeled stuff because we can't be sure who it is. In fact, don't follow anything unless you feel it totally from your heart.

The astral entities can themselves believe that they are angels, and they can tell you that, but they lie. They don't know they lie, but they lie. So, please read these channels' texts as stories and attitudes from someone or something very loving but not from Zoli's brain. I continue to wonder, if any of these beings are who they say they are or were. Could they be projections from my own various lifetimes? Possibly. Are they holograms from some way out-there place? From me in the future or the past? Or maybe from you? I don't know.

But they are loving and kind and tickle reality with vibrancy and joy.

<u>C'hin Lao..Listen To The Silence Within</u>

RP Journal Spring 1998

Some things can be learned but not taught. The unseen is perceived before it is recognized by the senses. That which cannot be taught but can be learned is done in silence. If you follow the dogma or teachings of a path, You live in the energy of that path. You will become the way of those who attend to that way by following the diet, the beliefs, by speaking the thoughts of the past teacher, so do you align yourself with that way. And, yes, you will grow and learn, but be cautious.

You will be dreaming the dream of another. Walking the way of another. Even if it is the way of a master, you must return again to this plane and find your own way. But do not worry. Do not rush yourself. It takes many lifetimes of walking the paths of the great ones to finally walk your own path to greatness. And what is that? Listening to the silence within, It is your final teacher. When you finally let go of all the ropes attaching you to dogma, to paths, and to gurus, You will appear to have no path at all.

You will be accused of selling out, of becoming too worldly, of missing opportunities, and so forth. K. You will, in truth, have become yourself. You may not look spiritual because you will not espouse the fashionable words of the times used by others who want to appear spiritual. You may, in fact, look like a total failure, a fool, but so what? If you have reached the center of the circle, you will not care of the opinions of those still spinning around in karma.

Find out what you believe by observing what you judge. Watch what bothers you

and follow it to the end by allowing curiosity to replace anger. Do not argue with your fears. Nurture them and let them flow through you And indeed, follow yourself.

Note: What would you do if you clearly saw a wizened Chinese man sitting on your couch one morning? I freaked. This was at the farm in 1998. The farm portals were like the Star Wars cantina in the movie. Beings from other places came in and out of these portals to rest.

I saw them a lot. They often told me stories or presented ideas that I was advised to research, to write down and keep them in a safe place. That went on for the twenty-five years I lived there. So, this Chinese dude said his name was C'hin Lao. He was very calm, very sweet, and quite detached. He, along with a bunch of other discarnates and higher 3D level folks, gave me most of the material I published in the Reality Pirate Newsletter.

Am I sure who they were? No, I'm not. But what I can promise you, though, is

that the writings were dictated from them to me by my furiously scribbling hand. The energy signature of channeled reception is quite different from those of the fourth chakra or above. I can't really explain it except it's very emotional. The differences are acute. I'm not a fan of anyone following channeled stuff because we can't be sure who it is. In fact, don't follow anything unless you feel it totally from your heart.

C'HIN LAO CHANNELINGS

<u>Beta Peptide: C'hin Lao</u>

RP Autumn Issue 1997

Question. What are the chemical changes occurring now in the body? Answer. The physical bodies of consciously developing humans are now creating new neurotransmitters in the neural area of said body. This means that the brain is having to find new ways to communicate what is going on to the body and to consciousness. Neurotransmitters are chemicals produced by the brain. They are messengers to the body. The old ones

have worked for centuries, but now that the veils are lifting, these neurotransmitters are not powerful enough to carry the increased frequencies of light to the conscious body.

The new neurotransmitter is called beta peptide. It is a synthesis of serotonin and a higher frequency of available energy that has been yet utilized by the physical body. Its advent into experience is accompanied by symptoms such as, one, increase in dream activity, two, nervousness, loss, or increase in sleep, three, confusion and panic, four, a sense

of being out of sorts. All humans on this plane are feeling these things to greater or lesser degrees.

If one has requested enlightenment, then he or she will feel more of an increase rather a quickening of the process than those who choose not to go so quickly. This is why some individuals appear to be crazed by the process and still others act like it's still the 1950s. Well, in their reality, it is. Try not to judge. Simply observe. Everyone gets there eventually. It's a personal choice. If you feel shaky and nervous, you may indeed request that the energies be tuned down a bit.

You may choose to slow your process to a pace you prefer. If you still feel some of the effects but to a lesser degree, we liken the nervous shakiness many of you feel to a Volkswagen bus speeding at a hundred miles an hour down a road. It shakes because it was not made to go at such a fast pace. It would require a major overhaul. In truth, if it could be transformed into a Porsche, it would well exceed even the hundred miles per hour which so stressed it when it was the bus.

And in truth, this is the process you now find occurring within yourselves. The new neurotransmitter will allow your transformation into a being who can handle levels of stress and increased frequencies of experience far beyond your present capacity. There is still a bit of a wobble going on as your so called old form shifts into higher gear of your so called new form. Portions of the body take longer than others to make the shift. These portions are ones you have created in illness and in fear.

Wherever you have attached greatly to an organ or a body part, so will that attachment hold density and disallow smooth transitioning. This is not a judgment, simply an observation. I hope this answers what you requested.

The Enchantress Of Ackmoor

RP Journal Autumn 1997

Let me tell you a bit about this story. I wrote this at my beloved farm in Olympia, Washington in 1997. I had many animals, Scottish Highland cattle, dogs, cats, a llama, several horses. Several of my dogs communicated telepathically with me. I was just learning this trick.

Why is it a trick? Because to this day, I'm not sure what really happened. I had a beagle blend named Chelsea and a yellow Labrador named Star helper. One day, as

I wandered through the pasture and Chelsea and Star followed me along with the other dogs trailing in the rear, I heard psychically, let us tell you about the Enchantress of Ackmoor.

I sat down, looked at the dogs, and felt the energy come through me. What the heck was happening? I don't know. I have since learned that in the far future, animals will be the communicators, at least some of them, from humans into the astral realms. I think many of us have this skill now. I am not unusual. But I'll tell you now what they told me. We are all

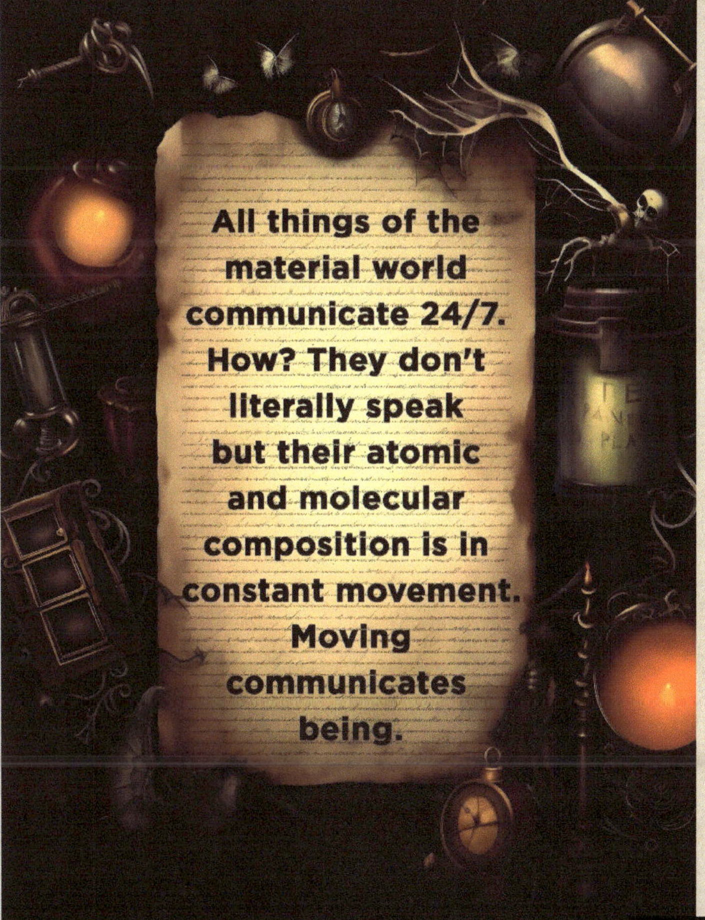

children of the creator. The great mysterious speaks through the forces and allowances of nature, inventing itself continually throughout the illusion of time and space.

We come to you now as simple servants of universal love. Our hearts ascend in the morning time of your consciousness when all life is pure and fresh. Our simplicity is our gift to you. Our knowledge is tempered by wisdom undivided by intellectual self argumentation. To sit with us in the peacefulness of your private space is to

know bliss. If indeed no physical animal is part of your life, my friends. Simply ask that one or many of us come to you in spirit to honor you as companions.

There are so many of us in spirit who desire to be near you all, yet we do not intrude. Ask for our assistance, our presence, and it shall surely occur. Let us now tell you a story about the Enchantress of Ackmoor. In a time and a place long gone from your now, there lived an old woman. Her family had died one after the other during plagues, famines, and wars. The village she knew as her home had been carted off piece by piece by those demanding more.

Livestock and pets, wildlife, and all living things had deserted this place. Indeed, the old woman knew loneliness. Her sustenance came from the ocean and bushes, and in the mild winters she partook of things she dried in the hot sun of summer. She passed her days feeling abandoned and bereft of friendship. The happiness she once knew was no longer even a memory. But one morning, an enormous wind rose up from the valley, a strange wind unlike one she'd ever felt in all of her hundred and twenty years of living.

This wind spoke to the old woman and said, "Enchantress, yes, you of great inner power and beauty. I have come because your dreams requested my presence. I have come to remind you of what you have lost." The old woman felt betrayed. Who had told this wind to remind her of her loss, her pain, and her loneliness. What cruel trick was the unseen now playing on her? As she continued in her anger, the wind again spoke.

"Enchantress, your loss is great, but these things you fear are not what I speak.

"Your great loss is that you have forgotten spirit. You lost your connection to God, your playfulness and your right to ask for help. Do you not desire to recall these things now?" And so it is true, she felt. Why had she not seen it before? All these past sixty years, she had felt only her loss of things and people and animals. Not once recalling her connection to spirit as her true source of life. Her eyes welled up with tears and her heart opened.

"Yes. Please help me," cried the Enchantress. "Tell me what to ask for because I, even I, have forgotten." The wind blew more gently now, unfolding the old woman in its caresses and whispering to her of the love and help ever available through the grace of the creator. "I feel for the first time in years," she started, "that I have a right to life, to love and what I live, and to honor myself. Oh, great wind, could you send me animal friends too? I so miss my companions."

The wind laughed and said, "done." All around the old woman now came a flock of brightly colored birds, dozens of small furry creatures, and an enormous smiling bear. The old woman's eyes shone with love and acceptance of the gift. She thanked the wind and asked if there was anything else she needed to do. "First,"

responded the wind. "Thank yourself, then allow these blessed creatures to lead you back to the creator. That is all." With a brush to her cheek, the wind left the old woman with her new friends.

For not only now was the enchantress happy, but she wanted to share her happiness with others. The animals and the old woman played in the sun and slept soundly under stars so bright they sent sparkles to land on the waves of the water. To this day, no one knows what became of the Enchantress of Ackmoor and her family, for the life they lived was so filled with bliss that the tiny island they called home ascended one night into the star full sky.

They still exist somewhere. Perhaps as you gaze out some evening into the beauty of the universe, you might see a beautiful island floating across the path of the moon. Perhaps it is so.

Walks With Horses

RP 1997 Autumn, Channeling

In the winter of 1994, I met and was adopted by an Indian woman in the Hunka Ceremony. She is and was Lakota Sioux. Her name is Kathy Boyd. In my Hunka adoption ceremony, I was given an Indian name. Soon after, I began channeling from native people in the world of spirit. Don't know why this happened, but I think I got a lot of good stuff. As usual, read this with caution.

Walks With Horses speaks. My name is Walks With Horses.

I am a friend of the Buffalo Man, Tatanka Woslai Nagin. He has asked that I come to you this night and speak to you of the sweetness of life. I'm an old woman. I draw the fish we catch in the cold river. I pick the fruit from the bushes along the mountain's feet and crush it with my own. I tend our goats and sheep. No one comes near. The wind believes my heart when I tell it I love it. The Earth mother, hears

my voice when I pray, and I send smoke unto the hills and to the great mystery.

I am a simple woman. When I was alive, I was these things. A medicine keeper, I was one of little trust in things seen and great faith in the unseen. I am Walks With Horses, keeper of the good way. If you follow your dreams, your destiny will allow you wisdom. If you choose trouble, then trouble will be your guide. Life's sweetness is all around you. The flyers, the swimmers, the creatures who crawl and have no hooves, all the four leggeds, and, yes, the two leggeds are filled with beauty.

I see beauty all around me. I sit now and watch the sun break fast over the hills. I sit and feel no confusion or fear because I am living my destiny. And what is that? Would you wonder if such a simple destiny, one with the company of goats, crows, dogs, for I am within my father's house? I sit always as his table of beauty because I know who I am. This is the sweetness of life. I am Walks With

WALKS WITH HORSES

Horses, friend to Buffalo Man who sends you greetings.

Hold your head high and fear not. For when I was this old lady, I met death, and it was like my life, a peaceful movement from the one fire to the next. Even though the wood was different, the flame was the same as before. And so it is now that I come to you. Bless each day and you will find peace.

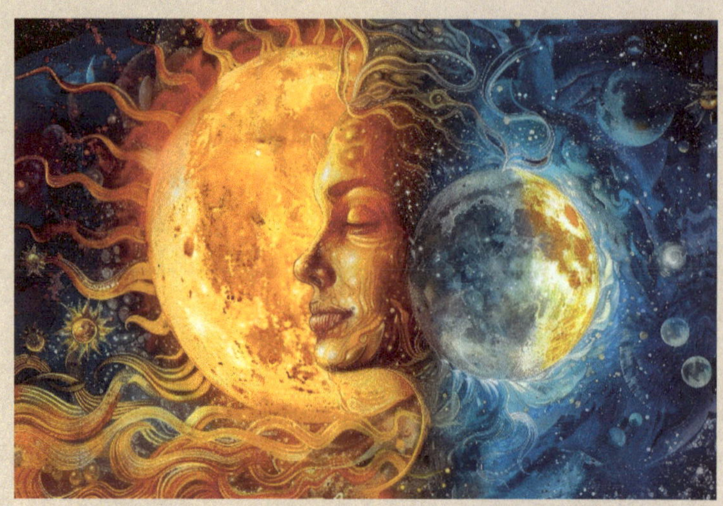

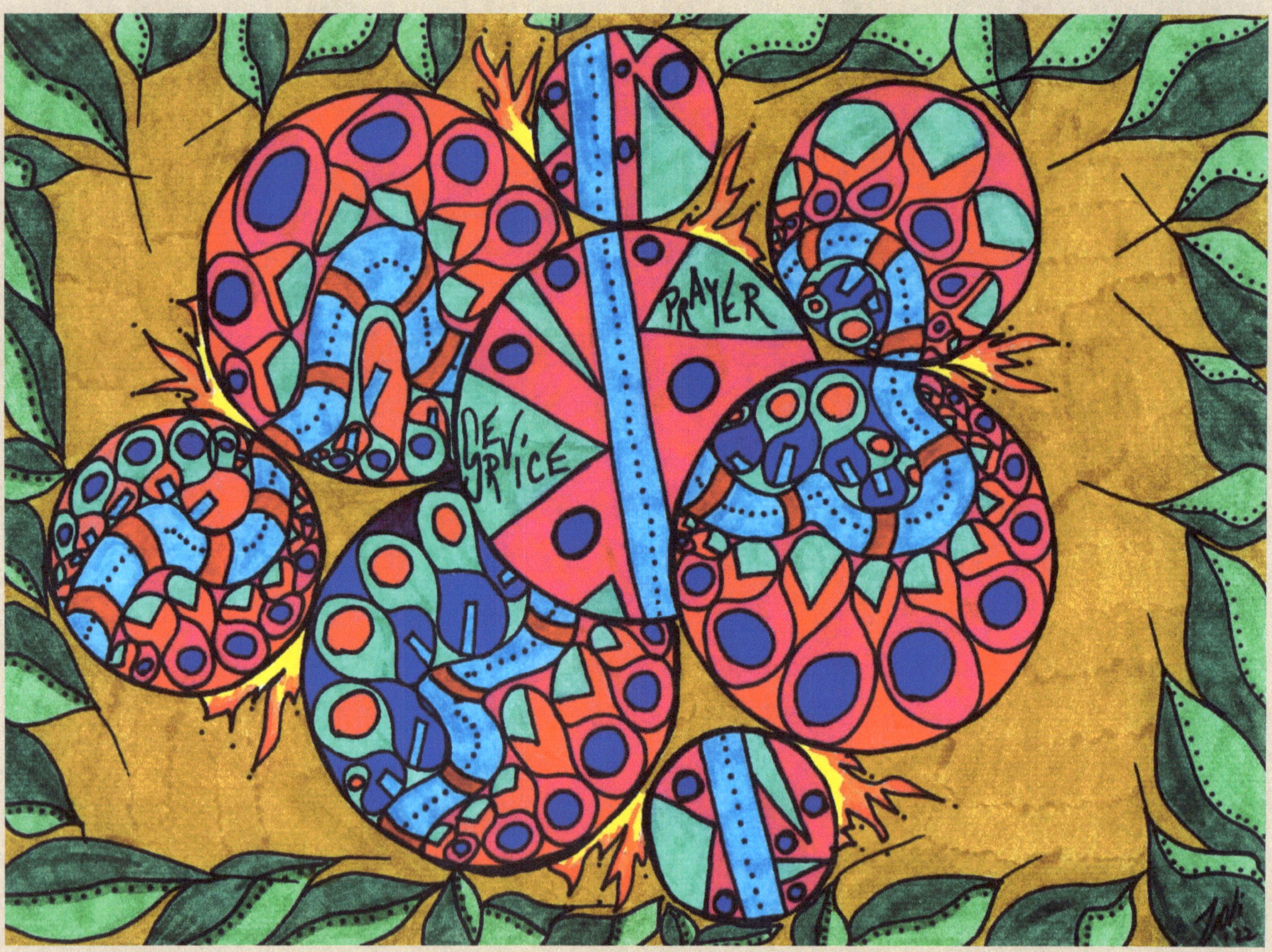

THE UNSEEN

If you look at a clock, it goes from twelve to twelve. When you go from 12:00 all the way around the clock to 11:50 or 11:55, that's all the unseen world. That little bit that left, that's all what is physical and seen. And that's why we get so confused.

We search. How can we not know who we are? We go through our whole life trying to find out who we are. That is so bizarre to me. How can I not know who I am, really, in the scheme of things? Well, you can't come into Earth life and know all that. That's the joke. That's what's hidden. And that is what we seek. That is the supernatural world.

The Beings that Guard and Guide Us, they have guide points, little stop signs and go signs. And if we learn more about ourself, how to be quiet through service and meditation and living a healthier life, those things will come more easily to us. And we can be a light in the wilderness for other people searching for it.

It's the most fascinating thing that we spend our lives searching for things. When I can't get the vacuum to work, I think my day is ruined. If I knew that there are universal forces keeping the Christ from talking, that might change my day.

There are some devastatingly destructive forces. And the problem with humanity is that the negative forces on this planet will shoot up into the lower first and second levels of the astral realm with all these conspiracy theories and negativity and hate, then sensitive people channel it down. They channel all that stuff about all the horrible things. The world is really horrible. It'll never change. And all this bad stuff's going to happen.

Plenty of bad stuff happens without making up more, but it's all because of greed. It's all because of the material world.

We're burning karma from all the stupid stuff we've done before, all of us. We're trying not to create new karma, which we do every time we open our mouth or interact with anybody. But what are you doing to make the world a better place? Stay in your lane. Do what's in front of you on a daily basis, your family, your home, your work, your community, your state of mind. That really works. It's not sexy and it's not dramatic and it's not Hollywood, but it works.

At different levels, there are beings who have it all figured out, but only within their own spectrum. The Masters certainly do. They've graduated from our school. They've got this whole thing figured out. But then what's coming next? We do live forever in one form or another. All that dies is this physical thing, these vehicles, these vessels.

Years from now, when the mystery schools open back up, when a child goes to a school, they will know their chart. They will know each child's point of evolution. They will know who and what they are and how to educate each child. You're not going to put a child who's a third degree initiate in a class with somebody who hasn't even taken the first because their ability to perceive things and their ability to do good on the planet will be different.

People will be nurtured in accordance with who and what they really are. Right now, it's not like that. It's horrible. And we can hope for that and know that it's a guarantee. That's exactly what will happen. The ashrams on the higher realms will be also on the physical once again. They were in Egypt. They were in

Atlantis. The mystery schools in Tibet, those things will be on the physical plane, and people will go there to learn things in accordance with their karma, the divine will, and their point of evolution, and what their ray structure is.

It's amazing because it's so radically different from the learning system now. But at the same time, the learning system now, people are starting to recognize it's not working because We the People, seven deadly sins, we can be greedy and we want a shortcut. And we lie to ourselves, then when we don't get it, we end up blaming that guru. Well, he told me if I did this and it didn't happen, so he's an asshole. No. You're an asshole. We can all be an asshole.

I just try to keep it real. I have made such an idiot of myself so often in my earlier years of training and channeling energies; I was going to ascend; and I was an alien. I wasn't. I've been through that. I've done it. I know why it's done and how we do it. But do it and get through it. It's a school. It's a class.

There are a lot of people who are seeking help and not finding it in the right places. And that's why I've written these

Chronicles. I'm hoping to get people to think for themselves and not give their life savings to a false prophet. There's too much of that going on. This is not about money. This is about thinking in different realities and seeing things from a different perspective.

I just like to say to folks, "Look, have you brushed your teeth today, maybe checked your finances? Talked to anyone you love? Have you tended to your physical life? How do you feel?" That's what counts. That's what really keeps us out of ourselves.

We're all trying to connect with the astral and talk to all these guys that are off world and meanwhile, we can't even cook dinner for ourselves. I have been there. I have done that. Oh my god, I lived that life. And it does nothing but just bring ego and eccentricity. You can be brilliant, but if you're eccentric, that's not good.

SUPERNATURAL INTERACTION

Satanic energy works through us, through people. Spiritual beings can also work through animals. They can appear and disappear at times, affecting the physical world. We ensouled beings are the ones that are transforming this planet. And that's where the interest lies. That's the center of the rainbow, so to speak. The beings that are in the astral realm are just like the physical in many ways.

just one way, and I can't even name how many ways there are to interact. Anything you can think is out there. Anything you can imagine is out there. When you look at Star Wars and the science fiction characters on television, where did those come from? I think those came from beings interacting with the physical minds of the people that wrote them.

Do we just make things up? No. We get help. So I think there is a constant interaction and a give and take. Part of understanding the supernatural world is finding how you interact with those beings. You will attract to you beings that are at your level and just a couple levels higher then you. You can help those who are just coming up below you the best.

It's all like the ladder theory. It's all hierarchical. Every bit of it is. So, the more conscious we are, the kinder we are, the more cleaner our life is, we will attract those beings. It's like walking down the street. You have alcohol stores, pot stores, and casinos on the left. And on the right, you have family entertainment or a bunch of dogs. You will go to whatever side you want to feed within yourself, and everything can become habitual.

And I'm not saying that going into a casino, you're going to end up wallowing in RP's hell. That's not it. There are no

real ideal things, but it's the repetitiveness of what we do and how we interact with these beings that makes a difference.

Now when you're interacting with lower astral beings or purgatorial spirits who died from suicide or drugs or whatever, you're going to enact that in your life too—as above so below. I didn't make that up, and you can't get past that.

That's just one of the laws of time and space in this world. You know the statement, misery loves company?

SUPERNATURAL INTERACTION

I like to say misery loves company and joy doesn't need any company because you are in a state of peace. You can have company. You can have like-minded others. But if you're miserable and doing lower chakra stuff all the time, there is so much guilt and shame and misery with that that you just don't want to be alone because it's scary.

That is the truth. And the people who I've met in my life that have been the most needy and unable to be by themselves are the most miserable.

Contributors

Thank you to the collaborators
who helped Zoli create and design
The Reality Pirate Chronicles.

**Photographic Art and Graphic
Design: Dreamstime.com**

**Editing and Layout:
Linda Beaulieu**

**Supernatural Beings Illustrations:
Christina Morrison**

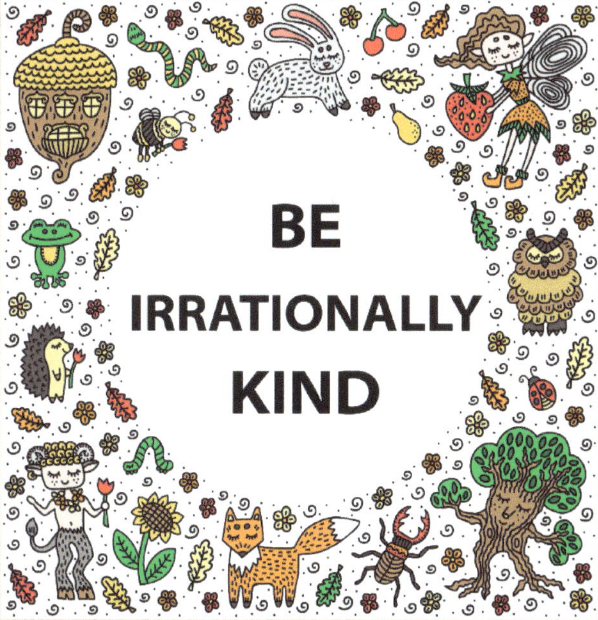

I want to express my gratitude to all you kind folks who have requested personal advice readings. I am beyond humbled by your trust in my assumed abilities yet report that I am unavailable to conduct personal readings, as my work remains focused on the collective. I cannot tell you how much your trust and confidence in the work presses foreword those of us at Zoliart to remain simple and work in integrity to the best our frail natures allow.

I compose these books and present videos for the expressed purpose of reaching as many folks as seek the work, not as a personal consultant or counselor. Humbly, all I can offer is on these sites. I present my own experiences as a researcher and encourage you to explore your own. Thank you.

Go in peace! Zoli Althea

Disclaimer

These writings and the content of this book are the property of ZoliArt Companies, LLC, its affiliated organizations and governing bodies, their members, managers, employees, agents or representatives (collectively, the "Owner") and represent the Owner's personal experiences and opinions. These writings and the content of this book are subject to copyright and may not be sold, transferred, copied, used, or reproduced in whole or in part without the prior written consent of the Owner.

These writings and the content of this book are neither legal, religious, medical, psychiatric, or psychological advice in any way, nor should they be interpreted as such if the reader chooses to adopt and employ any methods presented in this book. The information provided herein is general and not intended to address any specific issue or topic. The accuracy and completeness of information provided herein are not guaranteed or offered to

produce any results, and the advice and strategies contained herein may not be appropriate for any one particular person or situation. The Owner shall not be liable for any loss incurred as a consequence of the application or use, directly or indirectly, of any information presented in these writings. The Owner is not responsible for the actions or failures of any third parties, nor is the Owner responsible for any advertisements or for any content linked to this book. The Owner makes no representation regarding the reliability of this book. Readers accept all risks. Any claim for damages shall be limited to the amount paid by the claimant to the Owner for services.

©2024 The Zoliart Companies LLC

All rights reserved.

For entertainment purposes only.